The Hidden Assassin: When Clinical Lab Tests Go Awry

Alan H.B. Wu, Ph.D.

The Hidden Assassin: When Clinical Lab Tests Go Awry contain fictitious characters, events, and places. Any resemblance to actual persons, living or dead, business establishments, events, or locales is entirely coincidental. The science described in these stories, however, is factual.

ISBN-13: 978-0-9893485-4-6
eBook ISBN: 978-0-9893485-2-2

Dedication

This book is dedicated to my wife Pam, who is the creative force in me and believes that these stories need to be told.

Table of Contents

Prologue

****

This is a sequel to my first collection of short stories, ***Toxicology! Because what you don't know can kill you.*** In that book, I concentrated on cases where the results of drug and alcohol testing conducted in clinical laboratories played a role in the health and lives of many individuals. In this book, I have expanded the scope of clinical laboratory testing to beyond the testing of drugs alone. Clinical chemistry testing affects all of us from birth until death.

The Hidden Assassin: When Clinical Lab Tests Go Awry is an anthology about ordinary people's encounters with clinical lab testing. Something innocent like a blood glucose test can kill, or the finding of a chemical in blood can uncover a terrorist plot. Lab tests are also essential for determining the health of an unborn child. Genetic testing can now be used to determine if you are predisposed to get cancer or suffer a fatal side effect to a medication. We can determine if someone has suffered a heart attack or more importantly predict who will get one in the near future. The stories are based on true events. Because of patient privacy laws, the names and places have been changed. Reading this book might help you avoid the bad outcomes that happened to these people.

Clinical Lab Test Gone Awry

****

Judy, a licensed phlebotomist, made the mistake of showing the girl the large needle which she was going to use to collect blood from her. Francine was just 7 years old and could not remember having her blood collected before. When Judy came to her with the needle, she was terrified. A tear came to her eye and she cowered under her mother's shoulder.

"Mommie, do we have to do this?" She asked her mother.

"It'll be alright, Francine" she said to her. But her statements offered her little comfort.

"Please hold her arm out" Judy said to the mother. The phlebotomist was rather abrupt and impersonal. It was the end of a long day, and she had collected blood on nearly 30 patients. She wanted to go home and have dinner with her family. Judy was a large woman who towered over the small child. Reluctantly and with her eyes closed, Francine sheepishly held out her arm. Judy applied the blue rubber tourniquet under Francine's left bicep and began looking for the vein on the child's arm. Using her gloved finger, Judy flicked Francine's skin at the inside crease of the child's elbow with her index finger in hopes of teasing out the blood vessel. When she finally found it, Judy quickly inserted the needle. Feeling a tinge of pain, Francine screamed out, while her arm jerked away from the phlebotomist. This sudden movement caused the tubing to disconnect from the needle and blood started squirting out of the needle and onto the floor of the clinic. The bright red fresh blood provided a sharp contrast to the clean white tiled floor.

Holy shit! Judy said to herself. She placed a gauze onto Francine's bleeding arm and then grabbed a towel to clean up the mess. Upon seeing her own blood, Francine started screaming uncontrollably. Her mother tried to console her, but it was no use. Francine's blood test would have to wait for another day.

*

That unfortunate experience caused Francine to be afraid of needles for years to come. At first, Francine was very healthy and did not need much medical care and rarely needed to have her blood collected. That all changed when she was 16. In school, she was sitting next to a girl in class who was coughing and sneezing. The girl should have stayed home that day, but she was there to take an important test. She infected several of her classmates with the flu including Francine. Most of the other kids recovered after a missing only a day or two of school. Francine was not so lucky.

The day after the class, Francine was home with a

headache and fever. She was very thirsty and drank large amounts of water. She went to the bathroom every hour. After three days of no improvement, her mother called her doctor.

"Is she breathing fast?" the doctor asked.

"Yes" replied the mother."

"Does her breath smell funny or different?" was the doctor's next question.

"Yea, it smells a little fruity" she said. "And she is drinking a lot of water"

"Get her to the emergency room as soon as possible" he said. "I think she might be in a diabetic crisis."

But she is not a diabetic Francine's mother thought to herself hoping for the best but fearing the worse.

When the symptoms were described to the emergency department staff, a nurse came over and performed a bedside blood glucose test. When the mom told the nurse about Francine's fear of needles, the nurse assured her that for now, only a fingerstick collection would be needed. The nurse applied the spring-loaded device and it produced a small droplet of blood. Francine was barely awake and didn't move when the micro lancet cut her skin. The blood was placed onto the tip of a glucose strip and inserted into the measuring device. After a minute a glucose result of "455" appeared. The nurse knew exactly what was going on and immediately went over to the ER resident covering the case to show him the result.

"Let's get a blood gas, electrolytes, and urinalysis STAT"

he said to her. "Call the pediatric-ICU and see if they have an open room. Then call transportation and ask them to send an orderly."

Francine's mother was told that her daughter was seriously ill and needed additional blood work to confirm the diagnosis. Blood was taken from both Francine's artery and vein and sent to my lab for analysis. By that time, Francine was unconscious. A Foley catheter was inserted into her urethra and urine was taken. Within 10 minutes we called in a blood gas result showing that Francine was suffering from a "metabolic acidosis", a serious medical condition caused by too much production of acid by the body. One half hour later, we reported a low bicarbonate level confirming the acidosis, and high electrolyte values demonstrating that she was dehydrated. My lab's glucose level confirmed the result obtained at bedside. The finding of "ketones" in the urine completed the diagnosis. Francine was suffering from diabetic ketoacidosis. Francine's pancreas stopped working. Her inability to produce insulin caused her to have a dangerously high blood sugar level, essential for maintaining vital organ function. A sudden increase in glucose caused her liver to break down fat in her body resulting in the production of ketones as a byproduct. These breakdown products are acidic and cause the patient to exhibit a fruity-like aroma. High glucose also caused Francine to urinate excessively leaving her thirsty and dehydrated.

Francine was given intravenous fluids and an injection

of insulin which rapidly reduced her sugar to a normal level of 113. She was transferred to the pediatric ICU where she remained for a few days before making a full recovery. A pediatric endocrinologist was consulted on the case.

"Francine has insulin-dependent diabetes" the doctor told Francine's mother. "It was brought on by her viral illness, but she would have gotten this disease sooner or later. We're not sure why people get Type 1 diabetes, but there is a genetic link. She will require regular insulin injections. Her diet must to be carefully monitored. She will also be taught how to test her blood on a daily basis for glucose using a home device. Every few months, she must be seen at the diabetic clinic so we can see how she is doing. We will be ordering additional blood tests at that time. My diabetes nurse will explain what you and she should know going forward. She may need to give herself regular insulin injections. This is a very serious disease that can have significant consequences to her health."

Francine and her mom were told that diabetic complications include heart disease, vision loss, kidney failure, and permanent neurologic problems. Uncontrolled diabetics can lose limbs and die prematurely. Francine's mom started to cry.

"If she can control her blood glucose, we can expect Francine to live a long and meaningful life" the nurse concluded.

From that moment, Francine took control over her life and health. She was diligent in testing her blood and quickly got over her fear of needles. She also became obsessive about cleanliness, that would haunt her later. To her credit she never questioned why she was afflicted with this terrible disease. Francine got a teaching degree and became a high school counselor. She was very open about her diabetic status and welcomed meeting with students who also had this disease. She showed her students that diabetes can be controlled and that they could achieve whatever their goals.

*

While in her mid-twenties, Francine developed chronic pelvic pain, vaginal discharge, and pain upon urination. Her period also became irregular. After a few weeks, she went to see her gynecologist. A laparoscopic procedure was performed by the insertion of a small camera through her abdomen to visualize her pelvic area. The doctor saw inflammation of her fallopian tubes and diagnosed her as having pelvic inflammatory disease. While this is often caused by sexually transmitted diseases like chlamydia and gonorrhea, Francine was single and was not sexually active. Her infection was caused by excessive cleansing of her vagina which altered her natural flora. Microorganisms are normally present in all areas of our bodies, but Francine's repeated douching caused these organisms to relocate and infect her upper reproductive organs. Through the scope, the gynecologist also saw adhesions, which are fibrous bands that formed near her small bowel. The adhesions are often produced after abdominal surgery but Francine had no such history. In her case, they were caused by the pelvic inflammatory disease. Because adhesions can cause a serious small bowel obstruction, the gynecologist recommended surgery to have them removed.

Francine took a leave of absence from the school and scheduled the elective procedure. The surgery was without complications and she was admitted to the surgical intensive care unit. Among the treatments given to her was icodextrin. This is a polymer that keeps fluid inside the peritoneum to lubricate tissues and help prevent them from forming new adhesions. Because Francine was a diabetic, the staff paid special attention to her blood sugar levels. Surgery is highly stressful and causes an increased blood concentration of glucose. Francine's glucose level was checked every few hours using a bedside glucose meter. The hospital was practicing "tight glycemic control." Clinical studies showed that ICU patients have better recoveries if their blood glucose levels are maintained at normal limits through insulin injections. One of Francine's blood glucose was 350. Accordingly, an order was written by the nurse to give her insulin. The ICU resident noticed that Francine's previous glucose results were consistently within the normal range. Like a good doctor, he wondered why the result changed so quickly and questioned the high value obtained on the device.

"Hold off on the IV insulin and send a blood sample to the lab to confirm this high glucose result" he told the nurse. The resident knew that while the bedside glucose monitor is fast and convenient, it is not as accurate as the tests that we generate in the hospital's central lab. If our lab's result confirmed the point-of-care device, he would countersign the insulin infusion.

A blood sample was taken and sent to the lab and the test was ordered as stat. It normally takes about an hour for the sample to be labeled, delivered to the laboratory by courier or pneumatic tube, processed by the lab, centrifuged to obtain serum, given to the tech who loaded the sample onto the instrument, tested by the machine, and reported by the tech. It was at the end of the shift and both the doctor and nurse left the unit before our stat glucose result was available. The nurse from the next shift saw the insulin order. She obtained the insulin from the ICU pharmacy and administered the dose to Francine. Within a few hours, Francine's glucose concentrations quickly dropped to a dangerously low level as the result of the insulin she was given, and she fell into a deep coma. Her blood glucose read 22. Alarms went off on her bed monitor and at the nurses' station. ICU team immediately administered an intravenous glucose solution, but it was too late. Francine died of complications brought on by hypoglycemia.

In the laboratory, we reported a normal blood glucose level on Francine's blood. The value was very different from the value tested at bedside. In retrospect, we learned that some glucose devices produce falsely positive results in the presence of other sugars besides glucose. But where were these other sugars coming from? Francine was on intravenous nutrition. A search of the literature revealed that the starch icodextrin is broken down in the human body by pancreatic enzymes to sugars such as maltose. This maltose registered as glucose in the measuring device producing a falsely high value. Francine's actual blood glucose level was in the normal range, as confirmed by our test conducted in the laboratory. Our instrument and test method are not subjected to this interference. Once it was determined that we were using a faulty bedside glucose meter, the instruments were removed from the unit and replaced by newer devices that did not suffer from this problem. We sometimes take the accuracy of laboratory tests for granted because the vast majority of them are accurate. When they are inaccurate, it is usually due to a human mistake. In this case, a collection of isolated human and technological errors led to Francine's death.

*

The use of faulty blood glucose meters has caused erroneous glucose measurements resulting in the inappropriate administration of insulin. There have been over 100 deaths due to hypoglycemia. In addition to maltose, the presence of other sugars such as galactose and xylose can produce a falsely high glucose result. In 2009, the US Food and Drug Administration issued a warning to doctors about faulty test devices. In the ensuing years, these devices have been removed from the market but it was too late for Francine.

When the original studies on "tight glycemic control" were originally published in the early 1990s, it created a lot of excitement among ICU doctors. Many hospitals adopted this practice in hopes of improving clinical outcomes. Retrospective analysis showed, however, that this practice led to deaths due to low blood glucose, and the practice has largely been abandoned. Getting the glucose levels to fall within normal limits using insulin dosage adjustments has proven to be difficult. In the end, it is better to have a mildly high blood glucose level than a mildly low value.

This case also illustrates the importance of communication between healthcare workers between shifts. Today, before one group leaves a shift, they must meet, discuss, and document each case before the next shift begins. Compliance to "hand off" procedures are an important part of reducing medical errors and is one of the National Patient Safety Goals established by the Joint Commission, a regulatory organization responsible for inspecting hospitals for compliance.

Absence of Malice

****

Gertrude O'Malley was the stereotypical grandmother. There were always freshly baked cookies in the house. During the winter, she would occupy herself by knitting scarves and hats for all of her grandkids. When her husband died ten years ago of lung cancer, she devoted herself to her son John, daughter-in-law Lilly, and three grandchildren, all under the age of 12. She was very lucky that they lived nearby and came to her house on Sunday afternoons for dinner. She had a big yard and the kids loved to play in the field. When she turned 68, she started experiencing occasional chest pain when she did simple things like taking cookies out of the oven or walking outside to get her mail. Medical exams with her primary doctor revealed no risk factors for cardiovascular disease. She was not a smoker, although she was exposed to second-hand smoke from her husband for 30 years. She was not diabetic, did not have high blood pressure, and was not overweight. Although her cholesterol was slightly high, her "good cholesterol" was well above acceptable limits. Her doctor told her to take baby aspirin daily and to exercise moderately. This advice confused her a bit because she figured she got plenty of exercise chasing her grandchildren around the house almost every weekend.

On Labor Day, Gertrude planned a special day for her family. They all came over for a barbecue cookout. Her son John did all of the cooking on the grill while Gertrude made the salad and set the picnic table. Lilly was in the third trimester of her fourth pregnancy. Gertrude told her to sit, relax, and not strain herself as she propped her head up with a pillow. Around 10:00 that morning Gertrude began to experience chest pain. Unlike previous episodes, this time it occurred while she was simply sitting in the kitchen putting sprinkles on cookies. She didn't say anything to John because she didn't want to spoil the pleasant afternoon to come. This was typical of Gertrude. She never wanted to be a burden to anyone. After a few hours, however, she found the pain to be unbearable and finally told John about her symptoms.

"Mom, why didn't you tell me you were feeling like this?" he asked as he dialed 9-1-1 on his phone.

"I'm sure it's nothing, just like last time," she said while gripping the side of the table.

"Last time? You mean you've experienced chest pain before and didn't tell me?" John asked. Gertrude did not reply.

The ambulance arrived within 15 minutes. Luckily, due to the holiday, there was no traffic. They were at the emergency room at Parkford Regional Hospital within another 30 minutes.

It was 2:00 p.m. This was Gertrude's first trip ever to the ER. Lilly stayed behind with the kids. Once in the emergency room, Maria Johnson, the triaging nurse, proceeded to ask Gertrude questions.

"Mrs. O'Malley, are you having any pain right now?"

"Yes, but I can manage it. I don't know what all the fuss is about. I'll be fine," Gertrude replied, annoyed by this kind of attention.

The nurse continued, "Can you describe to me where it hurts and what you were doing at the time?"

Gertrude explained that she felt a sharp pain that centered in her chest but radiated out to her arms and shoulders.

Maria worked as an emergency room nurse for over 20 years at Parkford and had witnessed more than her share of heart attack patients. Gertrude's electrocardiogram showed all the regular signs and symptoms of a heart attack. Treatment for heart attacks has evolved over the years. Before, treating attacks was a matter of rest and using aspirin and anti-pain medications like nitroglycerine. Today, many patients are treated with acute cardiac catheterization. When medically indicated, a balloon is inserted into the coronary artery. When inflated, the balloon initially opens the vessel, allowing for vital blood flow. Once the vessel is opened, a stent – a thin, hollow cylinder of wire mesh – can be inserted to keep the coronary artery open. Maria knew that if Gertrude was experiencing a heart attack, time was of the essence.

While other hospital personnel obtained the necessary

identification and insurance information from John, Maria grabbed her blood collection kit. The doctors ordered cardiac blood tests STAT – immediately – and Maria labeled the tubes, took blood from Gertrude, and sent it to the lab. She also performed an electrocardiogram by attaching electrical wires to various areas of Gertrude's chest and side. The ECG showed some abnormalities, but the emergency department team could not determine if these abnormalities pre-existed or were new developments. To know for sure, they needed to review ECG recordings from Gertrude's previous visits to her doctor. A call was placed to her primary physician.

The laboratory performed a variety of tests on Gertrude's blood. The most important one was a test for cardiac troponin, a protein that is released into the blood stream after heart damage. After an hour, the test came back with a result of 0.04 ng/mL. According to the lab, this result was normal. Maria knew, however, that a single negative result was not sufficient to rule out a heart attack. The policy at the hospital was to collect a second blood sample at 6 hours and have it re-tested for troponin. Gertrude was ordered to stay in bed. John stayed with her. Her chest pain subsided with the administration of nitroglycerin.

"I feel fine now," she said to her son. "Can we go home? I want to be home with the kids."

"No, Mom," John said. "It's important for the doctors to complete all their medical tests."

Maria drew a second sample, at 5 o'clock, precisely 6

hours from when Gertrude presented to the ER. The new sample was delivered to the lab, again labeled "STAT". When the second troponin test result came back, the value was 0.06, just slightly higher than the first result, but still well below what would be expected with a heart attack. Maria went to consult the medical team in charge of Gertrude's care.

Dr. James Wilcox was the senior emergency department resident on duty. The attending physician, Dr. Marcus Thomas was available by pager. Dr. Wilcox knew that Dr. Thomas was probably having drinks at his country club on this Labor Day holiday after playing a round of golf, so he did not bother to call him. Dr. Wilcox went to see Gertrude to see how she was doing. He felt confident that the two negative troponin results were sufficient to rule out a heart attack. The pain may have been caused by indigestion or muscle pain. He signed the discharge order for Mrs. O'Malley, and John took Gertrude home.

In the car, John called Lilly to tell her that his mom was fine and they were on their way home. When they got back to Gertrude's house, John decided to stay over that evening just to be sure everything was okay. Lilly took the car and drove herself and the children to their home. The older two had school the next day. It had been a long day and Gertrude was tired. She excused herself and went to bed around 10 o'clock. She had no other complaints of chest pain. Satisfied that Gertrude was fine, John lay down on his mother's fold-out couch in the living room. It had also been a very stressful day for him, and he, too, quickly fell asleep. John woke up at 6:00 a.m. His back was aching because a bar beneath the thin mattress had pressed against his lower back all night. He stretched his arms, yawned, and then went first to the bathroom and then to his mother's room. Gertrude was normally an early riser, getting up every morning by 5:30 a.m. But there were no sounds coming from her room. She was not awake yet.

"Mom?" John said through her closed bedroom door. No response. He knocked and called to her again but with no success. He turned the doorknob and went in. Gertrude lay motionless on her bed. Her eyes were closed. There was no distress on her face. She was dead. John tried in vain to arouse her, hoping that she could be revived. But he knew she was gone. His shoulders slumped and his eyes started to tear up as he reached for the phone to call 9-1-1 again. This time, there would be no visit to the ER. After the call, he hugged his mother, kissed her on the cheek, and said goodbye. He left the room, and while waiting for the authorities, John called Lilly to tell her the sad news. The pathologist at the hospital determined that Gertrude suffered a heart attack that occurred in her sleep.

After the funeral, one of John's friends thought that Gertrude's death could have been prevented since she was in the ER just prior to her death. "Why would they discharge her if she was on the verge of that heart attack?" he asked. "Shouldn't they have kept her overnight for observation?"

John contacted Richard Shore, JD, Esq., a lawyer

specializing in medical malpractice. The medical and laboratory records for Gertrude O'Malley's case were subpoenaed and reviewed by John's lawyer. At Shore's advice, they hired me as an expert laboratory medicine specialist. Missing a diagnosis of "acute myocardial infarction" is the leading cause of medical malpractice lawsuits from the ER. The clinical laboratory plays an important role in the diagnosis of heart attacks.

*

My laboratory uses the same manufacturer of equipment used in performing the troponin test that was used on Gertrude's blood at Parkford. Very early in my career, I chose cardiac marker tests as my area of research interest. As such, I was involved with formulating national guidelines on how the troponin test is interpreted. Now, by carefully reviewing the data and timing of specimens relative to the onset of Gertrude's chest pain, I determined that she did not have a heart attack before coming to the ER. And since she was pain-free once in the ER, it was unlikely that an attack occurred after she arrived. While many missed diagnoses of heart attacks are due to the failure of ordering the appropriate tests, or misinterpreting test results once received, neither of these appeared to be the case here. I told Richard Shore that it was likely that Gertrude's fatal attack began while she was asleep at home that night. "There was no malice here," I concluded.

"Yet the patient died shortly after she was in the ER. She came expecting to receive good medical care. They should have predicted this outcome," Shore said.

"How can anyone predict when a heart attack will occur?" I asked, indicating that I disagreed with his assessment. The answer would come during the course of trial. Although they didn't ask for my testimony in court, I was kept on as a medical advisor for the plaintiff. Mr. Shore proceeded with the malpractice lawsuit. They sued Parkford Regional Hospital and Dr. Marcus Thomas, the attending physician on call that night, and the physician of record.

The risk management and medical teams at Parkford and a malpractice law firm hired for the case felt confident that there were no mistakes made in the handling of Gertrude O'Malley's case. So they did not settle the case and instead, it went to trial. John's lawyers argued that the medical team should have known that Gertrude was in danger and they should have at least kept her overnight in the Parkford emergency department. They brought in pictures showing a vibrant Gertrude having fun playing with her grandchildren. Shore said that these doctors have forever deprived these children of their "Nanny." The defense team argued that this characterization of Gertrude was prejudicial to the case and the judge sustained their objection. The defense brought in experts to testify that the physicians exercised established standard of care in Gertrude's case. Given that her symptoms had subsided, she was considered at low risk for a heart attack.

"Nobody could have predicted that she would die that

night," Dr. Thomas said on the witness stand. "We are not gods. We cannot predict mortality. Moreover, it is impractical to admit everyone who comes into the ER with chest pain who has been ruled out for a heart attack," he argued.

Richard Shore remarked to Dr. Thomas, "We are not suggesting that it was appropriate to admit everyone that night. Only Gertrude O'Malley."

At closing arguments, Richard Shore made a compelling argument regarding Gertrude's death. He introduced Dr. Samuel Johnson, an independent, expert cardiologist who stated that the change in troponin result from 0.04 to 0.06 was sufficient to indicate that something was about to happen. I did not agree with my own side's expert. I thought that this change in the troponin result could have been caused by the analytical imprecision in the testing. I met with Shore during the jury deliberation to explain my view.

"So are you saying that the results were not accurate?" Shore .

"No, accuracy and precision are different." To help him understand these important concepts, I explained an analogous situation as an example. "Suppose you are throwing three darts at a board. Accuracy is how close the darts are to the bulls-eye. Precision is how close the darts are to each other. If the three are close together but off target, you are precise but not accurate. In the lab, if you repeat a lab test you usually don't get the exact same result even on the exact same specimen," I said. "There is typically some fluctuation in the result."

"But we know what the truth is here. If the change in troponin results were not real, Gertrude should not have died" Shore replied.

I thought to myself, *Sure it is easy to conclude this after the fact, but does that mean it should have been evident to the doctors at the time? It was becoming clear to me that medical truth may be very different from medico-legal truth.*

While Dr. Johnson agreed with the other experts that Gertrude did not have her heart attack when she was in the ER, he went on to say that the attending doctors failed to recognize the impending short-term risk. In other words, it is insufficient today to simply diagnose, "it is also necessary to risk-stratify," Johnson stated. "Emergent exercise or pharmacologic stress testing could have been performed to determine if Gertrude's chest pain was of an ischemic etiology."

The judge asked the doctor to speak in lay terms.

Johnson replied, "Ischemic chest pain is a prelude to a heart attack and would be evident by stress testing. If the chest pain was due to some other reason, like muscle or joint pain, there would be no risk for immediate cardiac injury."

I was present at the closing, and later asked Dr. Johnson, "But wouldn't stressing a patient with ischemic symptoms be dangerous to that patient?"

Johnson replied, "If there is any evidence of cardiac injury by continuous electrocardiographic monitoring, the test is immediately stopped. Besides, it's better to have ischemia while you're in a hospital where medical care is readily available, than at home where there may be no one around to help. That's exactly what happened to poor Gertrude."

With Dr. Johnson's compelling arguments, the jury agreed with the plaintiff and ruled against Dr. Thomas and the hospital. Parkford's insurance group would have to cover the loss. I was surprised that my side won. Originally, I didn't think the O'Malleys had much of a case. Now that they prevailed, I wondered how this ruling would affect my laboratory practices. I hoped that our emergency department doctors were interpreting my troponin test results correctly. As I left the courthouse, I thought, "The bar has been raised when it comes to medical practices for cardiology. Even in the absence of malice."

*

Testing for cardiac troponin continues to be the standard for the evaluation of patients who present to the ER with chest pain. Increased analytical sensitivity for troponin assays has improved over the years to enable the detection of patients with minor heart injury. Risk stratification for future cardiovascular disease in the short term has become an important function of emergency department physicians, and troponin is used as part of that assessment. Making the best medical decision regarding patient management requires knowledge of test limitations. There continues to be confusion today as to how the results of troponin should be interpreted. In the past, when the test was positive, it indicated the presence of a heart attack. Today, the presence of any cardiac injury will produce a positive test, irrespective of the cause. While very high levels indicate an attack, a mildly increased level, such as that seen in Gertrude's case, indicates high risk for a future attack.

My mother recently experienced chest pain and went to the ER. I went into that hospital's clinical laboratory to see if the troponin test they were using produced high precision and sensitivity. With all that I'd learned from this case, I was determined that these doctors have the best information available in assessing the future for my mom.

Fatal Dedication

****

Shelly Wilson was an outgoing young woman who had steady employment as a marketing manager for a major pharmaceutical firm. Her job required her to do a lot of traveling. This made it difficult for Shelly to form any meaningful, long-lasting relationships. Although attractive, Shelly never married. She tried online dating services, but she was not able to find the right guy. She was an only child to parents who had her late in their lives. When they both died within a year of each other, Shelly, in her late twenties, was very much alone.

After fifteen years of working for the same company, she began yearning for something more in life. Over the years, she'd seen many of her co-workers leave to take jobs at other firms and relocate to different parts of the country. But Shelly was very loyal. The company hired her right out of college. She was grateful to them for giving her the job over other more experienced job candidates.

During one of her business trips, Shelly had a free

afternoon and was unsure how she wanted to spend her time. She'd seen all of the city's museums and art galleries, and she was not much of a shopper. So she just left the hotel room and wandered around downtown by herself. She grabbed a sandwich at a nearby deli and took it to the park next door to eat and watch the children play. After a half hour, a young man came along and sat down next to her. He was well dressed, clean shaven, and had a friendly face. He was wearing a name tag that read, "Toby, Ambassador in Training, The Holy Earth Revival."

They didn't speak at first, but then Shelly asked, "Pardon me; I was looking at your name badge. What is an Ambassador in Training?"

Toby replied, "I just joined the Revival and they are teaching me how to become a disciple. They just call us Ambassadors. They are training me to be a missionary so I can spread the Revival's word."

Curious, Shelly asked, "Who are the Revival and what do they stand for?"

Toby replied, "We are a group of people who believe there is a better way to live. We believe that people should lead natural lives. They should free themselves from social pressures and financial woes. They should eat organically grown foods without chemicals. We are vegetarians because we believe that all animals have a right to live and prosper. We respect all humans irrespective of their race, ethnicity, or social standing. We're basically an aid organization for the disenfranchised." Toby paused, and then said, "Wow, I didn't mean to give you a sermon. I actually just joined the Revival myself. I am sorry to carry on like this. I don't even know you."

"No, it's all right," Shelly said. "I was the one who asked the question. I respect your passion. Let's start over; my name is Shelly."

"I'm Toby. Pleased to meet you, Shelly. So what do you do?" Shelly explained that she was in town for business and had a few hours to kill before her dinner meeting.

After chatting for a few more minutes, Toby said, "My break is over; I have to get back to my training. It was nice to have met you."

"Good luck with your work, Mr. Ambassador," Shelly said. Toby chuckled and headed out of the park.

Shelly thought to herself that Toby seemed to have found what he wanted in life. If only she could do the same. She could not stop thinking about what Toby told her. Coincidentally, the next day, Shelly saw Toby seated in the lobby of her hotel. She tapped him on the shoulder. "So we meet again," she said. "Are you staying here?"

Toby turned around and smiled when he saw her. "Hi, Shelly! No, I'm meeting someone. Our headquarters are a few blocks away."

"I've been thinking a lot about what you said in the park yesterday" Shelly told him. "It made a lot of sense to me. How can I learn more about the Revival?"

"Why don't you come with me and meet the group? There's no pressure. We're friendly and are looking for like-minded people."

Shelly hesitated at first, but then said, "I'm going home today, but I come here every so often. So maybe I could come the next time I'm in town?"

Toby pulled out a card with the Revival's contact information and handed it to her. "I hope to see you again." And with that, they both moved on.

Once home, Shelly got busy with her job and did not think about the Holy Earth Revival. A week later, on laundry day, she discovered the card that Toby gave her in the back pocket of her jeans. She got on the Internet and learned more about the Revival. Many of their values resonated with her. There was a Holy Earth Revival branch in her town so she called and made an appointment to see them. They suggested that she attend the meetings, with no sales pressure or commitment to join. So she went to the lectures held in the evenings. Gradually she became more and more involved. After a year, the branch deacon asked her to enroll in the Ambassador training program at their headquarters. This one-week course was the same one that Toby attended earlier and could be completed during her vacation.

She signed up for the training program. Once there, she felt at home immediately. The people really cared about her. Toby was there and was delighted to see her. He became a full-time Ambassador, and turned over all his worldly possessions to the Revival. When her training was complete, Shelly decided that she too would give her life over to the group. When she returned home, she gave notice at her job and told everyone that she was joining the Holy Earth Revival. Her coworkers were shocked at the news. They considered the organization to be an extreme cult, especially when they heard about Shelly handing over all her savings. She assured them that she trusted the group's values and knew what she was doing. Tearfully, she said her goodbyes and left the office forever.

Shelly withdrew all of her assets from the bank and signed them over to the Revival. In return, the Revival would provide for her daily needs. She moved into an apartment at the headquarters location. She could marry but only to another member of the Revival. If she wanted to leave, she would be given $50,000 to start anew. Shelly was asked to go on missionary trips to rural and economically depressed regions of the U.S. She found these trips fulfilling. For the first five years, everything was great. She adjusted nicely to her new surroundings and responsibilities. Toby was a good friend and sometimes went with her on some of these missions. There was no romantic connection between them; she suspected that he might be gay. The Revival consumed both of their lives and there was little else to consider.

By the beginning of her sixth year at the Revival, Shelly started having doubts. She wanted to get married and start a family but wasn't sure how well that would work within the confines of the Revival. Other member couples had families, but when the children were of age, most left to start their own lives outside the group. If Shelly were to get married and have kids, she would not be able to devote the same amount of time to her work for the Revival. Over the ensuing weeks, she met with many of the group's leaders to discuss her doubts. They did not put any pressure on her to stay. "Everyone must find their own way," one of them said. "But you are doing great work here and we hope you decide to stay."

Another six months went by. Then Shelly fell ill. She had a fever, diarrhea, and a cough. She initially thought it was the flu. The Revival provides all medical care using only their own doctors. Shelly was confined to her apartment and given herbal medications. Revival doctors do not believe in pharmaceuticals, somewhat ironic since that's exactly what Shelly used to sell to doctors. Now, the Revival doctors convinced her that she would recover with a prescription of peace, quiet, and the removal of all stresses and responsibilities. But instead of getting better, she got progressively worse. By day three, she started hallucinating. She was put on a liquid diet, because she couldn't keep anything down. When Shelly started having breathing problems they finally called an ambulance. Toby was called and accompanied her to the hospital. She was taken to an emergency room that was 60 miles away, bypassing other hospitals on the way. The Revival wanted her to be seen by Revival doctors. When she arrived, her blood pressure dropped to dangerously low levels.

But the Revival doctors did not believe in giving her medications to stimulate her heart. Shelly was awake but unable to speak. Her eyes turned to Toby, who was visibly upset. She had the look of someone trying to say, "I'm not ready to go yet. Please save me." But she died within five hours of her arrival at the hospital.

In accordance with state law, Shelly's body was sent to the medical examiner's office and a complete autopsy was conducted. The attending pathologist found a blood clot in her left lung. A week prior to her death, she was in a car accident resulting in a severe bruise to her leg. A clot broke away from her leg and lodged in her pulmonary artery. The cause of death was listed as a pulmonary embolus. There was also an unusually high urea content in her eye fluid (vitreous). High urea in blood can be caused by dehydration.

*

Dr. John Harrison was the chief medical examiner of the county. He was trained at an Ivy League school and 35 years of experience as a forensic pathologist. He handled many deaths of notable celebrities in the region. His reports were always thorough and complete. He was well respected in the profession and had a spotless reputation within the media. His conclusions have never been seriously challenged in court. Given the publicity of how Shelly died, Dr. Harrison decided to examine the data himself. After extensive review, he reversed the conclusion rendered by his junior pathologist and signed out Shelly's death as caused by severe dehydration. He didn't give his junior colleague a reason for this reversal, which was highly unusual for him. Normally, he was very open about discussing cases.

The district attorney was contacted, and he filed charges against both the doctors at the hospital and the Revival for medical negligence. When the papers were issued, the Revival provided a document signed by Shelly stating that under no circumstances should Western medications be given to her, even in an emergency. The signature was dated from when she first came to the Revival and had not been updated. A statement was issued by the Revival to the local media: "Although Shelly Wilson's death was tragic and completely unexpected, and the Revival dearly misses her, the medical care given to her was in accordance with her wishes."

The DA dropped the case against the hospital, but continued the criminal case against the caretakers at the Revival headquarters where Shelly was staying.

*

I was contacted by the Revival to help defend their case. My lab at the University Hospital routinely performs the urea test in blood as a marker of kidney function. A disproportionately high urea concentration relative to creatinine, another renal function test, was likely due to dehydration. Normally, the serum electrolyte concentration, such as sodium or potassium, and protein levels are the best indicator of dehydration during life. After death, however, these levels are artificially altered due to postmortem changes and the natural degradation of proteins.

The use of urea as a measure of dehydration after death was usual, but the levels were so profoundly high that it was difficult to ignore.

I had no connection with the Holy Earth Revival, but was aware of the media's characterization that this was a religious cult. Nevertheless, I was only interested in the truth, irrespective of which side it might fall on. So I took the case. My job was to refute the cause of death as signed off by Dr. Harrison. While there was no question that the pulmonary embolus was present, was it caused by severe dehydration? If so, might that implicate the Revival as being negligent for not providing basic medical care? I reviewed the literature to determine if severe dehydration can precipitate an embolus. I found no such reports. Then I searched for similar death cases where the urea concentration was as high as seen in Shelly's autopsy. I found that her levels were higher than any level previously reported. I then went deeper into the testing procedures themselves, and learned that the urea concentration was measured months after death and not at the time of the autopsy itself. Could the levels have increased due to protein breakdown as part of the normal death process? Could the result have been contaminated by some outside source? Are there microorganisms that can produce urea as a byproduct? Could there have been other constituents that interfered with the test itself? I considered more sinister motives, by either party. Could there have been purposeful adulteration by the forensic laboratory with the objective of discrediting the Revival? Or did the Revival purposely do harm to Shelly because she wanted to leave? These conspiracy theories raised the stakes considerably for both sides. Unfortunately, I could not prove any of them. In my mind, the thought of opposing Dr. Harrison's findings would be a daunting task. I told that to the Revival's lawyers.

During depositions, the Revival hired private pathologists who reviewed photos of the body and compared them to the last photos of Shelly while alive. They saw no emaciation and weight loss as would be evidenced by severe dehydration. A postmortem review of her colon revealed constipation that was not consistent with severe caloric deprivation. Nursing records from the Revival's headquarters showed that she was given ample amounts of liquid supplements. I knew that the development of severe dehydration takes a week or more, not just a few days of deprivation.

It was beginning to look more and more as if the medical examiner was alone in his conclusion. Even his staff pathologist thought that Shelly's death was from natural causes. I asked the DA's office to investigate any past relationship between Dr. Harrison and the Revival. After a few weeks, an aide uncovered a lawsuit Dr. Harrison had filed against the Revival over some personal property rights some 20 years earlier.

"He may have a personal agenda against the Revival!" I told the aide. "In that case, he should have recused himself from signing the autopsy."

When Dr. Harrison was told that his previous lawsuit

was now known to the defense team, he reversed the cause of death. The final diagnosis listed by the original pathologist was restored. Now having no support from the medical examiner, the DA was forced to drop the charges against the Revival, and the case was dismissed before the trial began. Given the widespread publicity, this was an embarrassment to the prosecution and the medical examiner's office. The local newspapers had a field day. Under pressure from the county commissioner, Dr. Harrison was asked to resign from his post. He retired with full benefits, and quietly moved out of the area. He stopped writing, no longer attended professional meetings, and didn't respond to colleagues' attempts to contact him. He just went away.

Toby was distraught over the loss of his friend Shelly. He blamed himself for her death. Once the decision was made to go to the hospital, he should have insisted that she go to the nearest one, he now concluded. The extra few minutes could have made the difference. He hadn't realized that he really loved Shelly. Now that she was gone, his commitment to the Revival was waning. He left the Revival two months later and he, too, moved away.

*

Blood clots that occur in the veins of the leg are serious life-threatening events. They are caused by poor blood circulation, leg trauma, smoking, pregnancy, and prolonged immobilization. Individuals who take long airplane flights are at risk if they sit for many hours without getting up and exercising their legs. Some individuals have a genetic predisposition towards forming blood clots if they have mutations in coagulation factors. Clots that break away from the leg can lodge into the pulmonary circulation to produce an embolus. Some years ago, Derrick Thomas, an all pro linebacker for the Kansas City Chiefs was in a severe car accident and was paralyzed. Although he survived the car accident and appeared to be on the road to recovery, his immobilization resulted in a deep vein thrombosis several weeks later. This subsequently developed into a pulmonary embolus which resulted in his death. The Revival may have erred by not giving Stacey immediate medical attention once she began suffering from symptoms. Within a few years, Dr. Harrison, who was still a reasonably young man, in his mid-60s, died of natural causes.

Tree Trunks

****

Trudy Keene was overweight her entire life. She was diagnosed with hypothyroidism while in junior high school. She was told that this condition is associated with a reduced metabolism so that she was more prone to gaining weight than children with normal thyroid glands. Her pediatric endocrinologist prescribed thyroid replacement hormone in hope of improving her metabolism. But largely it didn't work, and she remained short and stout. Her adipose distribution was mainly centered around her hips and upper thighs. The kids in the neighborhood used to pick on her and call her "tree trunks Trudy." It hurt her feelings at first, but after a while, she learned to live with it. She would sometimes strike back by calling some kids "Pinocchio" if they had a large nose, or "Leno" after the light night talk show host, if they had a large head or chin. Over time, the kids accepted her as was and Trudy had a normal childhood.

Trudy attended the local University majoring in photojournalism. *I'm not attractive enough to be the subject of pictures,* she thought to herself, *but maybe I can tell stories about others through my work"* she thought to herself. Immediately after college, she got a job at a local newspaper as a photographer. Along with the reporters, she was sent to various locations within the city taking pictures of newsmakers and events. After 10 years on the job, Trudy left the newspaper and became a freelance photographer and writer. She always wanted to publish a book showing pictures of immigrants and telling their stories. She published several picture books that did well locally.

*

Across town at the medical school, Dr. Jacob Penfield was lecturing to his medical students and residents about the benefits of gadolinium contrast agents. Dr. Penfield is a recognized expert in the field of radiology, especially vascular angiography using magnetic resonance imaging or MRI. This technique enables a doctor to visualize blood vessels to determine if there is any damage or blockage.

"We are switching away from iodinated contrast agents to gadolinium" he said. In order to enhance MRI images, particularly for visualizing highly vascular organs, an opaque fluid called a radiocontrast dye is injected into the patient's blood before the scan is taken. "Iodinated contrast injection has the propensity to cause acute kidney injury in a handful of patients" Dr. Penfield explained.

"What is gadolinium?" one of Dr. Penfield's medical students asked.

"Gadolinium is an element from the lanthanide atomic

series found on the period table" Dr. Penfield explained. This resulted in blank stares from most of the students in attendance. While chemistry classes were a prerequisite for medical school, most of the students took these courses years ago and weren't chemistry majors. Neal Gerson was an exception as he was a chemistry major in college. Dr. Penfield's discussion reminded him of his advanced inorganic chemistry classes.

"Gadolinium has high absorption for neutrons and is therefore used to shield reactors" Neal said proudly. "The rods from the Fukushima crisis contain gadolinium." Many of Neal's classmates didn't like him because he came across as somewhat of a "know-it-all." But they held their breath because he was the senior resident.

"This same property makes it useful as a radiographic dye." Dr. Penfield stated. "The use of gadolinium chelates is not without its risks, however. Side effects have been reported when it is used in patients with pre-existing renal disease. We perform testing for serum creatinine as a marker of kidney function. From this measurement we are able to estimate the glomerular filtration rate, that is, the rate of blood flow through the kidney over time. The normal clearance rate is over 100 ml/min. We exclude the use of gadolinium agents on a patient when the creatinine level is high and the calculated filtration rate less than 30 mL/min. These patients are unable to remove gadolinium after our procedure and they become toxic."

*

A year or so earlier, my group in the clinical chemistry lab had a discussion with Dr. Penfield and his colleagues in radiology regarding our testing services for serum creatinine. This test of renal function is performed on virtually all of our inpatients and outpatients so we do tens of thousands of samples per year. Because kidney function can change rapidly, we always perform this test "STAT", with a turnaround time for reporting results of 1 hour or less from the receipt of the blood sample in the laboratory.

"We need a turnaround time for creatinine testing that is faster than one hour" Dr. Penfield told me.

Kidney function does not deteriorate that quickly, I thought to myself so I delicately challenged Dr. Penfield's statement. "Why isn't one hour sufficient?" I asked.

"We need to maximize the time that our patients are in our radiology suites and in our scanners. We cannot start a procedure until we have cleared patients for safety. It is very costly if our instruments are idle for even a few minutes" Dr. Penfield stated.

"Within the lab, we can reduce our turnaround time to about 45 minutes or so, but we cannot get you results any sooner than that. Samples have to be labeled, delivered, patient name and medical record number entered into the computer, barcode printed, sample centrifuged to obtain serum, delivered to the lab, put on the instrument, tested, results verified, and then reported" I explained.

"There must be a better way" Dr. Penfield said, somewhat exasperated.

"There are "point-of-care" devices that can be purchased and used in the radiology suite" I told him. "These devices are portable and reasonably inexpensive. But the results are not as accurate as what we can deliver from the lab."

"From a radiology point of view, accuracy is not as important as speed. We just need to get an idea if there is any evidence of kidney malfunction before proceeding."

"We don't have the budget to support the equipment and supplies needed for point-of-care testing as it is considerably more expensive than what we do in the lab" I mentioned to Dr. Penfield.

"Considering that it costs millions of dollars to have the MRI and CT scanning equipment here, the costs for doing creatinine testing is miniscule. We can take care of this from our budget" Dr. Penfield concluded.

Following this discussion, I went back to the lab and instructed my staff to investigate several point-of-care devices that can be used for creatinine testing. We settled on one device that used a dipstick test pad. Like home glucose testing, a drop of blood is placed on the stick and inserted into a measuring device. Results were available within a few minutes. The radiology department purchased the lab testing device, and we performed validation studies to compare it against our lab results. As I suspected, the dipstick was not as reproducible as our test in the lab. It is the clinical laboratory's responsibility to regulate all tests conducted on patients. We reluctantly agreed to allow the radiology department to use this point-of-care test in their unit even though testing from the lab produced more accurate results. However, we required that the individuals who perform the test are trained by our staff and their testing proficiency is evaluated on a regular basis. It is also important that test operators run "quality control" samples on a daily basis prior to their use on patients. These materials contain a known creatinine concentration, and are used to determine if the instruments are functioning correctly and the operators are getting the correct result. Dr. Penfield agreed to our terms and the test was made available within their MRI suite.

*

The radiology department trained many of their technicians on the proper use of the creatinine testing device that we selected. Patients who have an increased blood creatinine value are postponed or scheduled for other non-gadolinium dye injecting procedures. The radiology staff was diligent in performing and documenting the necessary quality control procedures. The availability of the device enabled them to better utilize their sophisticated radiographic instruments and personnel. Several devices were purchased and put into use. We kept a few extras in the lab that we maintained and rotated in and out of the radiology service, when maintenance of these devices was needed.

All went well for the first 9 months until Trudy Keene came into the General for an MRI angiography procedure. She had just returned from a photo-shoot in Southeast Asia for. Trudy developed pain and swelling in her left leg and went to our emergency room. She was also having difficulty breathing. The ER doctors ordered a "d-dimer" blood test from my lab. D-dimers are natural breakdown products of blood clots. Blood was also sent to my lab for a genetic test called "Factor V Leiden." Individuals with a mutation in this gene are at genetic risk for blood clots. Results of this test would not be available for a few days.

In the meantime, Trudy's d-dimer test result came out positive and she was diagnosed as having a "deep vein thrombosis," a blood clot in one of the veins in her leg. Of immediate concern to the ED docs was pulmonary embolism. This is when the clot from the leg breaks off and travels to the lungs through the circulation and blocks a pulmonary artery. Pulmonary emboli can cause chest pain and shortness of breath, and result in death.

Trudy was put on a gurney and sent to the radiology suite. As part of the protocol, blood was taken and tested for creatinine prior to gadolinium injection. The radiology technician was not immediately available to do the test, as he was assisting on another case. Dr. Neal Gerson said he knew how to operate the instrument. The quality control procedures had not yet been performed that day. The creatinine testing instrument has a "lock out" feature that requires performing these checks prior to use. Neal knew how to bypass this step. Because time was short, he performed the test without the quality checks. The creatinine result was normal and Trudy was cleared to proceed with the MRI. Trudy was given a special metal-free hospital gown and told to remove all of her jewelry. There was a concern that her hips were too large to fit into the MRI machine but there was just enough room, and the angiography was conducted. The result was negative for a pulmonary emboli and she was sent to a hospital bed. She was given a prescription for warfarin, a blood thinning drug used to prevent future blood clots, and discharged the next day.

Within a few weeks after the procedure, Trudy legs began to have pain and swellings again. She thought that she was having another episode of deep vein thrombosis and went back to the ER. She was given the result of her Factor V Leiden test which was positive, indicating that she is a high risk for blood clots.

However, this time, the skin on her legs was hard and tight, with dark red patches. Trudy was referred to a dermatologist for evaluation. Given her recent history of an MRI scan with gadolinium, he immediately ordered a serum creatinine. The result came back abnormally high suggesting an impaired kidney filtration rate. Ultimately she was diagnosed with "nephrogenic systemic fibrosis" due to gadolinium. The appearance of skin has been described by some clinicians as resembling the bark of a tree.

I was called to investigate how this could have happened. We examined the records of the creatinine testing device on the day of Trudy's procedure. While there were no flags or error messages when Trudy's test was conducted, there was a malfunction on the next sample tested and the device had been taken out of service. My heart skipped a beat when I saw that quality control procedures had not been performed that day. We eventually learned that Dr. Gerson had conducted the test on a device that was not functioning correctly. He was reprimanded for his inappropriate actions. It was a lesson he learned at the expense of Trudy. We were obligated and willing to report this incident to our internal quality management board as a medical mistake. Corrective actions were taken to prevent a similar occurrence. This report was made available to our Hospital's accreditation body when they came for an inspection. Trudy was treated with steroids which relieved her symptoms and offered some benefits. Her kidney disease was also treated and returned to normal.

Trudy could have initiated a lawsuit for the adverse outcome she suffered. After speaking with Dr. Penfield and other hospital administrators, she concluded that this was an honest mistake and was satisfied that this wouldn't happen again to anyone else in the future. She accepted our apology and did not bring us to court. In her concluding statement, she remarked, "this is not the first time someone has called me "tree trunks

Trudy."

*

In 2007, the Food and Drug Administration issued a warning to the radiology profession regarding the dangers of using gadolinium contrast dyes on patients with a glomerular filtration rate of less than 30 mL/min. This was issued because the agency received over 250 cases of nephrogenic systemic fibrosis (NSF). They noted that there were no reports of NSF when gadolinium was used on patients with normal renal function. In 2010, the FDA issued a requirement to gadolinium dye manufacturers requiring a labeling change to their product.

Testing for renal function whether from a lab or point of care is now standard with use of these dyes. Prior to the adoption of standards for creatinine testing, there were none. In one report, there were no cases of NSF among 53,000 MRI cases with gadolinium enhancement, including 6,000 cases where the GFR was borderline, i.e., between 30 and 60 ml/min. One way to minimize NSF is to use the minimum dose needed to perform the imaging. In Trudy's case, an error in the measurement was made that produced a falsely low creatinine result, and a falsely high filtration rate. Thinking the patient was safe, the radiologist gave her the full gadolinium dose for imaging.

Trudy learned that individuals who are on long distance airplane trips are at risk for deep vein thrombosis. Being a big woman, it was not easy for her to get up and stretch her legs while in flight. Patients who have one copy of the Factor V gene mutation have a 5-7 fold higher incidence of developing a blood clot. Those with two copies of the variant gene have a 25 to 50 fold higher risk. Trudy possessed two bad copies and was at the highest risk. Knowing this and having a prior history of deep vein thrombosis, Trudy made a point in future long airplane trips to walk the aisles and do leg exercises. The warfarin was vitally important to prevent a future blood clot.

Taking Its Toll

****

It was her first one. And it was particularly difficult. She did all the right things in preparing for this. The exercises and stretching, the breathing, and the psychology of it all. She was diligent in attending all the classes. At the end, she had a lot of confidence going in. Her partner, Millie was there too, every step of the way. Millie had not gone through this before either, so it was the first for both of them. During the early months, she did not gain a lot of weight. In fact, most of the colleagues at her two jobs didn't even know about it until about 60 days before it happened. She was in great shape, and at 25 still very young. But it turned out to be a lot more difficult than she could ever imagine. She had never been in real pain before; no broken bones, no accidents or prior hospitalizations. She even was able to keep all of her wisdom teeth. But now she was screaming. Her shouts echoed throughout the ward. I never understood why these units don't have more padding on the walls. Why can't someone invent noise cancelling devices? Sort of anti-yelling to cancel out human yelling. It would really come in handy for some professional tennis matches. For the staff, this was business as usual. They had heard much worse. To them, it was sounds of their profession. Like a football player hearing the crunch of shoulder pads. Or the soft taping of feet by ballet dancers during rehearsal. For them, it was even therapeutic. They didn't want muffling. This is how it is and has been since the beginning of mankind, um, or rather womanhood. Anyway, another was just about ready to come into the world.

"I got to have it!" She cried. "Tell them to give it to me now!" She was sweating profusely. Her hair was matted down against her scalp. She was squirming uncontrollably while Dr. Diane Mackowitz was examining her.

"Calm down Roma. We said we weren't going to need this" Millie said, holding her hand while standing next to her in the birthing chair.

"I don't care now. I can't bear it any longer" she cried.

Dr. Mackowitz replied. "You're 9 centimeters now. The child is coming. But if you need it, we can give you the epidural."

"Do it. Do it now!" was Roma's response. "Please?" she pleaded in a softer voice.

The anesthesia resident was summoned. He asked Roma to bend over so that he could gain access to her back. He felt her vertebrae with his bare fingers to locate just the right spot.

Roma felt his cold fingers, but she didn't care. When he found the right spot, he removed a sterile alcohol gauze from its package and wiped her skin clean. Then he took a small syringe from his tray and injected lidocaine, a local anesthetic, just below the top layers of her skin. Within a few moments, she had no feeling there. Then a larger needle was inserted into the epidural space just outside Roma's spinal cord. The needle was removed and replaced by a tube connected to a syringe containing bupivacaine, which was slowly infused into Roma's cerebrospinal fluid. Within a few minutes, Roma's demeanor changed completely. She was now calm and composed. *I'm ready for the next chapter in my life* she thought. She profusely apologized to Millie and the medical staff for her behavior. She had never been that out of control before.

The nurse told her that no apology was needed. "Honey, you're having a baby. We all understand."

Roma's pregnancy was unremarkable from that point forward. The Lamaze technique was just not for her, but nobody could predict that. Roma delivered a boy. They knew through a prenatal ultrasound exam that Roma was carrying a male. She and Millie decided to name him Julius. Upon examination at birth, the pediatricians at the General Hospital noticed that Julius had some structural birth defects.

*

Millie and Roma was a lesbian couple. Millie was 12 years older than her partner. Millie was Roma's high school

English teacher. Roma loved her and knew it wasn't just a crush by a high school student for her teacher. Millie sensed that there could be a connection too but was very careful in not expressing her feelings towards Roma while she was still a student. But a few years after Roma's high school graduation, they became friends and eventually, Roma moved in with her former teacher. By then, Millie was in her mid-thirties. She always wanted children and was sensing that her biological clock was at the 11th hour. *This may be my last chance to have kids of my own,* she thought. Now that she was with Roma, she started talking about having a child with her.

"I love you Millie, but I am unwilling to be with a man in order to conceive" she confided one night. "The very thought repulses me."

"There are other options" Millie said. "What about *in vitro* fertilization?"

"Where would we get the sperm from?" Roma asked.

"There are anonymous sperm donor banks. While the names have been permanently stripped of the samples, they do maintain a database that includes among other things, the health and ethnicity of the donor" Millie explained. "But the cost of *in vitro* fertilization is very expensive. There might also be a stigma associated with a lesbian couple having their own child."

Roma shouted, "I don't care what others think! We love each other and the rest of the world will just have to get used to us having a kid. Nobody at school seemed to care when you came out of the closet and told them you were with me?" Millie's statement regarding the societal implication of their situation appeared to hit a nerve with Roma, and motivated her. "Let's do it."

Because Roma was much younger than Millie, they agreed that Roma was best suited to be the egg donor and carry the baby to term. They knew that birth defects increase dramatically with advancing age of the mother. Millie and Roma went to see Dr. David Ming, a clinician specializing in vitro fertilization. They were shocked at how much the procedure cost. None of this was covered by Millie's insurance policy from the school. While both of them had the same thought, Roma was bold enough to comment.

"Are you sure you are not jacking up the price because we are lesbians?" was her question.

"We do not discriminate in providing medical services. That is against the law. I am professionally insulted by that comment. Please leave my clinic" was Dr. Ming's comment and he got up to leave them.

Millie immediately spoke up. "No, please, doctor. Roma didn't mean that. She is young and sometimes doesn't think things through before she speaks. We would very much like to be your patient. Can we please continue?

Dr. Ming looked at Roma's eyes and felt that she was sincerely sorry for that inappropriate comment. After a pause, he agreed, and they formulated a plan. Through the injection of hormones, Roma's ovaries will be stimulated to produce multiple eggs. Then a needle is inserted through Millie's vagina and into her ovaries to retrieve some of her eggs. The eggs are examined and the best ones selected for fertilization with fresh sperm from a donor. The fertilized egg is observed in the lab for 5 days prior to implantation into Roma's uterus. The entire cost of this procedure is $15,000. Millie and Roma didn't have the money necessary for this expense. So they told the doctor that they would return in a few months to initiate the process once they saved enough money.

Millie's salary as a teacher was sufficient for her and Roma to cover the expenses for her apartment and meet monthly expenses. Roma never went to college and worked as a cashier at a local diner. In order to save up enough money for the *in vitro* fertilization procedures, Roma took a second job as a ticket toll taker at the nearby turnpike. The work was boring and tedious, but it brought in the extra money they needed to pay for their medical bills. After a year, they went back to Dr. Ming.

*

The toxicology laboratory at the General Hospital was able to acquire the latest mass spectrometry equipment to perform routine and emergency analysis for drugs. It became apparent that this equipment could also be used to examine blood and urine for environmental toxins. We are affiliated with the University and have an obligation to conduct medical research. One of my students, Dr. Gerald Woodruff was interested in the field of environmental toxicology. The relevant chemicals in the environment included plasticizers which are used to make plastic products more pliable, flame retardants which are chemicals that are used to treat furniture fabrics so they don't burn as quickly in a house fire, and bisphenyl A or BPA, a chemical used to make plastics and epoxy resins. BPA is found in many household items such as water bottles, thermal paper used in printing computerized receipts, and as a resin for tin cans used for store food and aluminum cans for beverages. Our research effort was trying to link the concentration of BPA from blood and urine samples to the presence of clinical disease. Through our studies and those of others, it was determined that BPA as a chemical mimics the physiologic effects of estrogen, a naturally occurring hormone found in women. The toxic effects of BPA are most pronounced in infants, young children, but especially fetuses. High concentrations of BPA present in a pregnant woman exposes the growing fetus to this chemical. This can result in significant developmental problems for children. For girls, it includes a hyper-responsiveness to estrogen leading to infertility, advanced puberty, and accelerated and sometimes altered breast development. The adverse effects of BPA for boys is different. Very different.

*

Julius was born with cryptorchidism; he had no testes in his scrotum. Radiology images showed that they were still inside his body cavity, right next to his kidneys. This was not a major concern to the pediatricians. In the majority of cases, the testes descend down to their natural position within 3 to 12 months. Julius also had hypospadias. This is a birth defect where the opening of the urethra is altered from being at the tip of the penis to below the tip and even down the underside of the penile shaft. On Julius, his urethra opening was located at the mid-section of his organ. Millie and Roma were horrified to see these defects. The doctors told them that the cryptorchidism will likely correct itself and the hypospadias could be surgically repaired when he is a little older. This greatly relieved the women, and they took Julius home a few days after his birth. What the doctors didn't know was that Julius' anal genital distance was considerably shorter than normal children. This was not a measurement that was routinely done then or today.

At 18 months of age, Julius's testes did not descend down to his scrotum. His doctors decided to do an operation to repair both the hypospadias and cryptorchism. The surgery went without incidence. After it was over, Millie said to Roma, "finally, he can be a normally appearing boy."

By the time Julius entered preschool at age 3, it was evident that his behavior was different from the other boys. He opted to play with other girls and favored "nurturing" toys like dolls over "aggressive" toys like guns and trucks. Millie thought that this was natural because there was no male in the family. Perhaps he would grow up to be gay which didn't bother them either. But this was the beginning of differences between his childhood and a normal one.

By the time he was 10, Julius asked his parents if he could have a sex change operation. He always felt that he should have been a girl all along. Millie and Roma then initiated long discussions regarding his "assigned" gender, but it didn't change what he believed was right. Sex change operations are not performed by surgeons at this early age. Millie and Roma were counseled to have Julius undergo an endocrinology analysis by Dr. Casey Colander.

Dr. Colander did a thorough physical exam on Julius, focusing especially of his genitals. Julius was asked to wear a gown and to remove his undergarments. She asked Julius to lie on his back with his legs propped up and spread apart. Julius was embarrassed by this but knew it was necessary. Dr. Colander lifted Julius' gown and got out a small ruler. She measured the distance between his anus and the base of his penis. She recorded the distance and asked him to get dressed. She then went into the other room where his parents were waiting. Once he got dressed, Julius was asked to wait in the outer office.

"What was your occupation when you were pregnant with Julius" she asked Roma.

"We could not afford the in vitro fertilization at first so I worked two jobs; a cashier and I collected money at a toll booth" Roma responded.

"Did the restaurant use a manual credit card machine where a receipt is generated by swiping paper across the card?" Dr.

Colander asked.

"No, we used an automated credit card machine, where there was a printout that customers signed."

"What about the toll both, did you have to give drivers receipts and were they printed on thermal paper as well?"

"Yes, we were one of the first at highway traffic control to use these printers. What does this have to do with Julius?" Roma asked.

"I'll get to that. Do you normally drink bottle water from plastic container?" Colander asked.

"Yes, it gets hot in those toll booths, so the highway gave us unlimited amount of bottled water. I was always thirsty and drank tons of water."

"Was the water stored in a refrigerator or left out at room temperature" Dr. Colander asked, but already suspecting the answer to this question.

"There was no room for a refrigerator in our tiny toll collection booth. They were exposed to the sunlight" was Roma's response.

"This is all making sense" Dr. Woodruff said. "Although I cannot prove this, and it really doesn't matter now, I believe that during your pregnancy, you were overexposed to a chemical called bisphenol A. This is found in plastic water bottles. Water bottles that are exposed to heat accelerate the removal of BPA from the plastic container itself. BPA is also one of the chemicals used in thermal paper that you handled."

"What did this do to Julius?" Millie asked.

Dr. Colander took a pause then responded. "Julius has a shortened anal genital distance or AGD. When children are exposed to endocrine disrupting chemicals in utero, their AGD is reduced in both girls and boys. Clinical studies have shown that shortened AGDs in boys have a higher likelihood of suffering from fertility problems as an adult" she said. "BPA may have disrupted Julius' endocrine system before he was born. This could also explain why he had the other birth defects when he was born." Dr. Colander had access to Julius' complete medical record.

"But why me? There were other pregnant girls who worked in the toll booths" Roma asked.

"You may have a genetic predisposition towards this condition" Dr. Colander responded. "If you are a slow metabolizer of BPA, the amount you were exposed to may have stayed in your body longer than for other women. This is new research that we are still learning about."

"Is there a way to test this Doctor?" Millie asked.

"We can check your BPA levels now to see where you stand today. But if you are not planning on any more children then you should be fine."

Blood and urine samples from Millie, Roma, and Julius was taken and sent to my lab for analysis for BPA. All of them had normal ambient levels of this chemical. Roma is no longer exposed to high concentrations of BPA, as she no longer works as a cashier or in a toll booth. She and Millie never had any other children. A few years later, they were able to find a surgeon who performed a transgender sex operation on Julius. He became Julia and was a happy and content young teenager.

*

The health effects of bisphenyl A are suggested through epidemiologic studies. No one can be certain if there is a direct cause between birth defects and BPA exposure. The "feminization" of behavior for boys exposed to BPA in utero has also been suggested by population studies, but a randomized trial to prove this notion has not and cannot be conducted for ethical reasons.

BPA has been in commercial use since 1957. Roughly 2.2 million tons were produced in 2009, with the majority of it used to make polycarbonate plastic. The increased need for BPA was created by the bottle water industry which uses this form of plastic. There have been concerns by the US Food and Drug Administration regarding the hazards of BPA use for pregnant women, fetuses and infants. This has led to a ban on the use of BPA in baby bottles. As of 2012, 28 states in the US were considering legislation against the use of BPA. If BPA is removed, an important question will be the toxicity of the BPA replacement, e.g., bisphenyl AP, B, C, E, S, etc. If these alternative chemicals also prove to be endocrine disruptors, the safety of our unborn children will remain in question. Perhaps the removal of all plastics may be part of the solution. This will help our environmental issues as well since plastics require 500 to 1000 years to degrade in a landfill. Alternative renewal and biodegradable materials may be the solution for the next generation.

The Phantom Pregnancy

****

Cindy Hobart had been an elementary school teacher for the past nine years. She started out teaching kindergarten, but voluntarily transferred to an eighth grade class. She felt that these kids were a little more challenging and required a lot less babysitting, although that wasn't always true for some of the boys in her class. In any case, she loved children and couldn't wait to start a family of her own. Cindy was married to her high school sweetheart, Michael. They lived in a small apartment near the school where Cindy taught. Since they only owned one car, Cindy walked to school each day. Michael worked as an assistant manager at Target, a local department store.

Cindy was now in her mid-thirties and was concerned that she could not get pregnant after many years of trying. She watched her diet, did not drink alcohol or smoke cigarettes, and maintained her physical fitness. She kept regular visits with her gynecologist, Dr. Wendy Robbins. Dr. Robbins suggested that Cindy and Michael visit a fertility clinic to see if there was anything physical that prevented them from conceiving. All the tests came back negative for both of them. The fertility specialists told them to be patient and keep trying.

Cindy was told that in hope of maximizing their chances of conception, they might benefit from using over-the-counter fertility and ovulation blood tests for menstrual cycle hormones that fluctuate during the month. A follicle stimulating hormone test is taken within three days from the start of the menstrual cycle. A value too high or too low might indicate a lower likelihood for conception for that month. Cindy took the test at the right time and the result came out normal. So far, so good. In the middle of her menstrual cycle, she took the luteinizing hormone test to determine when she was ovulating. She took this test for several consecutive days waiting for a positive test result. When the hormone appeared, she would call Michael to come home early for a romantic evening. When none of these things appeared to work, they began to think about adoption. They didn't have enough money to consider in vitro fertilization. Cindy's menstrual period was very consistent, so, when her period was two weeks late, she was cautiously optimistic. Although the drugstore's urine pregnancy tests were negative, she knew that they didn't typically show a positive result immediately after conception. So she made an appointment with her gynecologist. Dr. Robbins' nurse drew blood from Cindy and sent it off to the laboratory for a serum pregnancy test. Dr. Robbins used the clinical laboratory at the University Hospital. She did her residency there and was familiar with its operation. A few days later, Cindy got a call from Dr. Robbin's office. Her human choriogonadotropin, or "hCG" test was positive. She was pregnant! It was June and she was on her summer break from school. She rushed over to Target to find Michael to tell him the news face-to-face. He was in the hardware section when he saw Cindy rushing over to him with a big smile on her face.

"What's happened?" he asked.

"I just got the news from Dr. Robbin's office. We're pregnant!" Hearing the news, Michael lifted Cindy off her feet and cheered. At last, their dream of having a family was becoming real.

Then, fully realizing the impact of her words and that he might be hurting her, Michael quickly put Cindy down and said, "Wait! How do you feel? You should sit down. What can I get you? Do you need me to boil water?" He was kidding, of course.

Cindy said, "I feel perfectly fine, honey. Nothing's happening yet. Relax. You're going to be a dad." With that, he picked her up again and spun her around.

Dr. Robbins scheduled a series of regular appointments with Cindy to monitor her pregnancy. She underwent regular testing of hCG to monitor the growth of the baby. Later, ultrasounds were conducted. Cindy was lucky that she didn't suffer any early side effects from her pregnancy. No nausea, morning sickness, or pain. Everything seemed normal. As if she really wasn't pregnant. On the third visit with Dr. Robbins, Cindy got the bad news. The pregnancy was not going as expected.

"In a normal pregnancy, your hCG should increase at a dramatic rate. We have now done three levels on you, and your levels have not changed," Dr. Robbins explained. "By now, using our latest ultrasound techniques, we should have been able to find a gestational sac in your uterus or somewhere else in your body. So far we haven't been able to find one"

Cindy was stunned. "What does this mean, Dr. Robbins?"

"These data indicate that you are probably not pregnant. The most likely explanation now is that you have a tumor that is producing the hCG that we are detecting in your blood. This can be very serious and life threatening. I didn't tell you before because I wanted to be absolutely sure. But we must now take immediate action. Fortunately, I believe it is still early in your course. And you have an excellent chance of...."

Cindy was no longer listening. All she knew was that she wasn't going to have a baby. She ran out of the office, while Dr. Robbins was still in mid-sentence. She went into the bathroom and broke down; tears smeared her makeup. After a few minutes she grabbed a towel and wiped her face. She left the medical building and drove to Target. She found Michael in the back of the store and told him the horrible news. Michael told the store manager he needed to leave with his wife and they went home. They didn't say anything in the car. There was nothing more he was going to get out of her. She was too upset. Michael put Cindy into bed, turned off the lights and left the bedroom. He then called Dr. Robbins who confirmed what Cindy told him. He wanted to make sure Cindy heard it right. But there was no doubt in Dr. Robbin's mind.

"There must be some mistake," Michael said to the doctor. "Cindy has been in perfect health her whole life. She rarely gets sick and has never spent a single day in a hospital."

Dr. Robbins then said, "There is no mistake, Michael. We had multiple blood draws on Cindy, and we retested the last sample just to be sure. It's time for us to make some difficult medical decisions."

A conference was held among Dr. Robbins, Cindy, and Michael. "Gestational tumors are life threatening," the doctor explained. "They can grow very rapidly. We can avoid the complications of cancer by removing the uterus as soon as possible. I have consulted my colleagues who agree with this approach." Michael agreed that Cindy's life was more important than having a baby sometime in the future and convinced her to proceed with a total hysterectomy. The operation was scheduled toward the end of the month. Cindy told the school that she needed a one-year leave of absence. The surgery went without complication. However, Cindy underwent regular chemotherapy to ensure that the tumor would not come back. She lost all of her beautiful long blonde hair. She was physically weak and lacked energy. She became very depressed and was medicated with antidepressants, which didn't work for her. She rarely left the house except for therapy sessions. Cindy's world collapsed. Michael tried his best to console and comfort her. But he was slowly losing the battle.

A month after her hysterectomy, Dr. Robbins performed a repeat hCG on Cindy. This is typically done to determine if the tumor has been eradicated. Much to her surprise, the result came out positive again, and at about the same level as it was before the surgery. Dr. Robbins did not understand how that was possible. The hCG in Cindy's blood should have declined dramatically. Dr. Robbins picked up the phone and called me. I went back to the lab and found Cindy's last blood sample. The other samples from several months ago had already been discarded. I instructed one of my senior technologists to add an antibody blocking solution, and the sample was retested for hCG. This technique enables us to test for an antibody interferent. A reduction or elimination of the hCG result would confirm is presence. When the test was completed the next day, I called Dr. Robbins.

What I told her came as a shock to Dr. Robbins. She was upset and angry at the same time.

I explained to Dr. Robbins that some individuals harbor unusual antibodies in their blood that interfere with certain tests. "Does Cindy have a history of suffering from any autoimmune disease?" I asked Dr. Robbins. "Or do you know if Cindy was exposed to any mice or small rodents? For example, did she work in an animal research lab?"

Dr. Robbins replied, "No, she has no prior history of

any disease and doesn't work in a lab. She is an eighth grade science teacher. Wait, her class does dissect mice each year instead of the usual frogs. Is that important?"

I explained that Cindy may have developed mouse antibodies, which were interfering with the hCG test. Since the test itself uses mouse antibodies to recognize the hCG protein, the presence of anti-mouse antibodies mimics the analyte even in its absence.

"We have a procedure to check for the presence of mouse antibodies. After you called, I had the lab check Cindy's specimen for mouse antibodies. The test came out positive. Cindy has HAMA, a human anti-mouse antibody. This was the reason the lab produced a falsely high hCG result."

"You mean this was a stupid lab error? How is that possible? We repeated this test on her three times before her surgery." Dr. Robbins was livid and began shouting at me. "If you knew of this phenomenon, how could you let this happen? Why wasn't I warned about this? How come you don't test every sample for the presence of interferent? What are YOU going to do about this?"

I kept my cool while defending my laboratory practices at the same time. "Dr. Robbins, I am sorry that this happened. The hCG test is only approved by the FDA as a marker of pregnancy, not of gestational tumors. We issued a warning a few years back when a false positive test result occurred on another lab test. If you look at the original lab report on Cindy, it shows that we noted that hCG results are not to be used for diagnosis of tumors and that heterophile and HAMA antibodies can cause false positive results. It is an uncommon occurrence, so we do not test for the presence of HAMA antibodies on every sample." Dr. Robbins looked at the report and saw the footnote indicating these warnings.

She then said, "How can you expect us to read all of this fine-print crap. What am I going to tell the family?" I wasn't expected to answer that question, and we both hung up. Dr. Robbins knew that this would not be the end of the story for her or her practice. I knew then that Dr. Robbins and I would not have a cordial relationship again from this point forward.

Dr. Robbins asked Michael and Cindy to come to her office, and explained that a terrible mistake had been made. Cindy was never pregnant nor did she have cancer. The operations and chemotherapy were all unnecessary. Moreover, because of her hysterectomy, she would no longer be able to conceive a child. The good news was that she was expected to live a normal and long life. Michael was relieved knowing that Cindy's life was not in danger. But he knew that a big mistake had been made and they would be paying for it for the rest of their lives.

"I'm sorry, Dr. Robbins, but we'll be contacting our attorney on this," Michael said.

Dr. Robbins responded, "I understand, you do what you must." Cindy sat quietly in the chair without any words, head down. Michael took Cindy by the hand and they left the office.

Michael explained the circumstances of his wife's medical care to an attorney who was part of a well-known law firm that specializes in medical malpractice lawsuits. They decided to separately sue Dr. Robbins for the wrong diagnosis, my laboratory for providing the wrong result, and Chase Diagnostics, the manufacturer of the hCG test. My lab was exonerated because we provided a warning on the laboratory report. I provided several papers that described the problem, and further showed that my lab was following standard procedures used in laboratories throughout the U.S. Chase Diagnostics also previously documented the potential problem and printed an appropriate warning in their package insert. They noted that other manufacturers have similar problems with their tests. Their lawyers knew that they were a legal target because they were a big corporation with a lot of money. Chase Diagnostics wanted to avoid the negative publicity that this case could have brought against their test. As the industry leader for clinical testing, the company felt it was in its best interest to offer the Hobart family a substantial settlement for its part in this tragedy. There was a stipulation made that no blame was to be placed on Chase Diagnostics. The Hobarts accepted the settlement offer.

The case against Dr. Robbins went to trial. Part of the defense's plan was to blame Chase Diagnostics for producing a faulty test. Had Cindy's test been accurate in the first place, none of the ensuing things would have occurred. Dr. Robbins' lawyers also tried to put some blame on the Hobarts, for not requesting a second opinion regarding the need for surgery.

"This is typically done for major surgical decisions," the defense attorneys stated. Michael could not believe that they were trying to blame him and Cindy.

"We put our trust in you," Michael said at the trial while looking directly at Dr. Robbins. "We had no reason to doubt your judgment. You said that time was important and that it was necessary to have this operation right away." Cindy was present in the courtroom but was not asked to take the stand. Michael thought it would have been too much for her emotionally to testify. Their lawyer did ask Cindy to appear in court without her wig so the jury could see what Dr. Robbins and the chemotherapy did to her. Their lawyer also made it perfectly clear that with the hysterectomy, there now would never be a chance for Cindy to become pregnant. After both sides stated their closing arguments, the jury was asked to deliberate. When the jury returned, after just four hours, the foreman announced that they ruled in favor of the plaintiff. Dr. Robbins and her attorneys decided not to appeal this decision. With this and the Chase Diagnostics settlement, Michael and Cindy were financially secure. Michael and Cindy both quit their jobs. They decided to use some of the money to establish a fund at Cindy's old school to renovate the school's library. The library was named after Cindy, their former teacher. Cindy would have gladly traded the settlement to have children of her own and her old life back.

Cindy Hobart never got over what Dr. Robbins did to her. She never went back to teaching. Her relationship with Michael also suffered irreparably. Michael didn't feel that Cindy was emotionally ready for or capable of adoption. Even after many years of joint counseling, Cindy's attitude toward life did not improve. Michael longed for the days when Cindy was loving and caring. They got an amicable divorce, splitting their assets equally. Michael moved out of town and eventually remarried. Cindy took her share of the money and moved into an apartment on the outskirts of the city. She had no friends and rarely went out. She became a recluse.

*

This and other phantom hCG cases have alerted the clinical laboratory, obstetrics, and cancer communities to the limitations of laboratory tests based on immunoassays. hCG is not the only test that suffers from this type of interference. False positive results for cardiac troponin, used in the diagnosis of heart attacks, have also been reported. While manufacturers have improved their assays to reduce the likelihood of antibody interference, it is impossible to construct a fool-proof test. What I've learned about medicine is that there are always exceptions. Therefore, it requires a vigilant medical community to question results and seek advice and other opinions when laboratory results appear discordant with clinical presentations.

Medical malpractice lawsuits against obstetricians have become a major issue in the United States. The rising costs of malpractice insurance has resulted in many doctors limiting their practices to *gynecology alone. Award limits for malpractice lawsuits have been instituted in some states. This has become necessary so that there will be somebody to deliver our babies in the future. In California, the limit is $250,000 for non-economic damages. In Pennsylvania, award limits are constitutionally prohibited, which has led to a shortage of obstetricians in that state.*

In God's Hands

****

Carol grew up and lived on a farm her entire life. She came from a very large family of 10 brothers and sisters. Many of them still live within 30 miles of her. When she married Hank Christenson, it was natural that she too would have a large family. She was 16, he was 34. They were both hard-working farmers from the Bible Belt. Carol was a strong woman. She was now a little overweight from having given birth to so many children: seven boys and four girls, whose ages ranged from 4 to 26. There was one set of twins. Carol and Hank did not believe in contraception. Therefore, when kids came, it was by the grace of God.

The Christensons believed in an honest day of work, which began at 4:00 a.m. and often didn't end until well after dark. They didn't care about money. Family was the most important aspect of their lives. On Sundays, the whole family was off to church in their Sunday-best clothes. Carol and Hank owned a grain farm. They grew corn and soybeans. They also raised cows for their milk and chickens for their eggs and meat.

Each day there were many chores to be done.

Carol was in charge of the house, feeding and clothing everyone, and making sure everyone got a good education. She home-schooled the younger children until they were 12, then they were ready to go to middle school and beyond. Carol made sure that all of the younger children helped around the house.

Hank was in charge of the farm and the family's finances. The older children helped with the farm work. Many of them planned to stay in the area and become farmers themselves. Some went, or were planning on going, to college, where they would learn how to improve crop yields, pesticide use, and disease resistance with hybrid seeds and genetic engineering. As much as possible, Hank Christenson tried to do things the old way. The way his father and his father's father had done.

The oldest daughter, Kayla, wanted to get away from the farm. She was a good student, finished college, and went to law school. She joined a practice in town, not far from her parent's farm. Not married yet, Kayla came home frequently to visit.

Carol got pregnant again. Having so many children before, she knew right away and didn't need any laboratory tests to tell her. She announced it to Hank by saying, "Pappa, 'nother one a comin'." He nodded to Carol and went on with his business. By this time, Hank was over 60. He thought of a lyric from a Beatles song he'd first heard as a teenager: "Nothing's gonna change my world." It was over four years since their last child and Carol was now 43. Kayla was concerned for her mom's health. Kayla told her that birth defects occurred more frequently in women over 35. Carol didn't want to discuss her pregnancy with Hank, Kayla, or anyone else in the family. It was her personal business. She was always healthy and with God's help, this child would be fine also. But Kayla convinced Carol that she should at least see her obstetrician for more prenatal care than she was given with her other children. They went to see Dr. August Summer, who delivered most of Carol's children.

At the office, a young receptionist told them, "We don't have a Dr. Summer here, ma'am."

Carol replied, "What do you mean? Most of my kids were delivered by Doc Summer."

One of the nurses in the room behind the receptionist overheard the mention of Dr. Summer and intervened. "Mrs. Christenson. It is nice to see you again, dear. Doctor Summer retired three years ago. The receptionist is new and didn't know him. Dr. Penny Albertson has replaced him. Let's make an appointment for you to see her next week."

Carol and Kayla came into the office the following week and were seen right away by Dr. Albertson. She asked, "Mrs. Christenson, what makes you think you're pregnant?"

Carol responded, "Honey, when you've had as many as I have, you just know."

Dr. Albertson responded, "Let's take a look." She examined Carol, took her blood pressure, felt around her tummy, and asked her for a urine sample. The office owned a small laboratory, where a urine pregnancy test was conducted. To no surprise to Carol, it came out positive.

"I'm 15 days into this Dr. Albertson. My old man and I don't get it on too often anymore. But he was frisky a few weeks yonder."

"Momma!" Kayla exclaimed, very embarrassed. "The doctor doesn't need to hear all the details."

"Never you mind child, maybe you should go back to the waiting room."

When Carol returned for her next appointment four weeks later, she was by herself. Dr. Albertson performed an ultrasound and drew blood for a quantitative human choriogonadotropin or "hCG," a hormone that is produced during pregnancy. The blood sample was sent to a lab across town. Dr. Albertson asked Carol if there were any issues with her pregnancy. Carol responded that she was spotting some blood.

"Why didn't you call me about this?" Dr. Albertson asked.

"I've bled before," Carol responded. "So I didn't think it was a problem."

Dr. Albertson saw that the ultrasound showed some thickening of the endometrium. She was not able to visualize a gestational sac. She feared that Carol might be carrying an ectopic pregnancy, a fetus that is growing outside the womb. These pregnancies do not go to full term. Dr. Albertson knew that if an ectopic pregnancy's gestational sac broke open, it would be a serious and life-threatening medical emergency. Dr. Albertson did not tell Carol any of her suspicions so as to not worry her. But she did ask to have another blood sample taken from her two days later. Dr. Albertson's nurse gave Carol directions to a blood-drawing station, where blood could be taken from her and sent to the lab for a repeat hCG test. Carol agreed to do that, and left the office.

The following week, Dr. Albertson got the results of both hCG tests. The first one was 2800 and the second one, 48 hours later, was 510. Dr. Albertson's believed her initial suspicions were correct. She called Carol and Kayla into her office. She explained, "In a normal pregnancy, the hCG result should double every two days. I have the results from your lab test. Your hCG result dropped dramatically instead of increasing. I am afraid you are carrying an ectopic pregnancy." Dr. Albertson went on to explain what that was and how it happened. If a fertilized egg gets implanted in the fallopian tubes instead of the uterus, it can cause an abnormal pregnancy such as this. The incidence increases substantially when the mother is older than 35.

Carol responded, "But I feel fine. I'm sure everything's all right. Why don't we just wait and see Doc?"

"No we shouldn't wait," said Dr. Albertson. "These sacs can break open and can be very painful and cause significant medical complications." Dr. Albertson told Carol that she should undergo a chemical abortion with the injection of a drug.

"But we don't believe in abortion. I won't do that."

Dr. Albertson explained, "This is not an abortion. Your pregnancy will never come to full term and you will lose the baby anyway. This drug only accelerates the natural passage of the fetus without the risk of a rupture. You won't feel any pain with this medication."

"Momma, please do this. I don't want anything to happen to you. "Kayla pleaded with her mother. With considerable reluctance, Carol agreed to have the treatment.

Carol was asked to return to the phlebotomy station later that week for a repeat hCG. A day later, she came to see Dr. Albertson for a progress report. Dr. Albertson conducted an ultrasound and reviewed the hCG report from the reference laboratory. She was expecting a further drop in hCG values and was shocked to learn that the value went up to 8000. The ultrasound revealed a uterine sac. Carol was still pregnant; it was not an ectopic pregnancy. Thinking it through, Dr. Albertson came to the conclusion that the second hCG result must have been in error. Neither Carol's pregnancy nor her life was ever in danger. Given this news, Carol was relieved.

"So I'm gonna have this baby after all," she said, smiling. But there were no smiles on the faces of Dr. Albertson and Kayla.

"You don't understand," Dr. Albertson said. "We have started a highly toxic drug that should have terminated your pregnancy. We didn't complete the treatments. Now it looks like you have a viable pregnancy. But unfortunately, it is likely that your baby, should it be delivered, may have significant birth defects. We recommend that we continue the abortion treatment..."

Carol jumped up and said, "No. I've had enough! I've listened to you once and look what you have done. From here, we're going to let Mother Nature take over. Whatever the consequences!" Kayla tried to reason with her but knew she would not be successful. She and Carol went home.

*

In anticipation of a medical malpractice lawsuit, Kayla started an investigation as to how this could have happened. She didn't tell her mom or anyone in the family. I was contacted because I had previously published articles on hCG testing. Kayla explained the situation to me and I agreed to investigate the possibility of medical malpractice. I knew the director of the lab who performed the hCG testing on Carol's blood. Richard Gardener worked for this lab for 20 years and was well respected in the clinical laboratory community. He and I knew each other from various scientific meetings. Rick went back to the files and found no problems with the instrument or the quality control records performed that day. These synthetic control materials contain known amounts of hCG and are tested along with samples from patients. In order to verify that the instruments were functional that day or any day, the hCG results from these controls must be in a predetermined range. I determined that since Carol was carrying a viable pregnancy, her repeat hCG should have been 5600, a doubling from the previous result, not the 510 result the lab reported. So I asked Rick if there was another sample with a result at or about this level in among the batch of samples tested on that run. Rick looked but found that all the samples run that day were completely negative. None of them could have been mixed up with Carol's specimen. Rick asked who collected the sample. I told him that it was a drawing station that was owned by Rick's lab. Therefore, even if there was a mislabeling, Rick knew that his company would still be responsible. After some additional investigation, Rick and I concluded that the instrument must have malfunctioned on Carol's serum sample. The machine may have failed to pick up the required amount of sample. A clog in the plumbing might have caused less of the serum specimen to be tested than expected. This could have resulted in a falsely low hCG result on Carol's blood. Chemistry instruments have sensors that look for these types of problems, but they are not foolproof.

I reported these findings to Kayla and told her that the laboratory must have made an error. The three hCG results were not consistent with one another.

Kayla asked me, "In your opinion, who was most culpable, the lab or Dr. Albertson?"

I replied, "Both parties made a mistake. The clinical laboratory made a mistake in providing the wrong test results, perhaps an instrument malfunction. There was no human error or negligence that I could see. Dr. Albertson made a medical decision based on what she thought was true and accurate. However, the final responsibility of any medical decision rests with the physician. Dr. Albertson needed to be sure in her assessment of an ectopic pregnancy, given the potential consequences of a wrong diagnosis. It would have been simple to have re-ordered the test and gotten a new result." Kayla also contacted other obstetricians for their opinions regarding how her mother's case was handled. All agreed that there were mistakes made and that there were grounds for a civil suit.

Carol continued her pregnancy to term. A month before her due date, she delivered a baby girl. The newborn didn't cry when spanked. The child was small for her gestational age. Apgar scores were 3 and 4, indicating that the baby was not completely normal. She was missing a left hand and exhibited other anatomic malformations. Carol named her Hope. She was hospitalized for the first two months of her life. It was obvious that Hope was not developing normally. She didn't meet milestones for her age. Kayla knew that this was the result of the cytotoxic drug given to Carol during her pregnancy. She waited for six months and then told Carol and Hank that she was investigating the circumstances of this case.

"Momma, I think we should sue Dr. Albertson and the clinical laboratory for medical malpractice. This shouldn't have happened to you. We can get a settlement for medical costs and to help you raise Hope. She will likely need special attention."

Carol was outraged. "This is not your concern, Kayla.

Hope is my child. I know how to take care of her. I took care of all of you and you turned out all right."

Hank, who was quiet during this entire ordeal, finally spoke. "Honey, this is not our way. God has given us baby Hope. We are in His hands. Everything will be fine. We are not interested in a lawsuit." He then left the room. There was a tear in his eye, but he didn't let Carol or Kayla see it. Kayla knew that this was the last word. She never brought up the subject again.

Hope did have a difficult childhood. She had seizures, was mentally delayed, and was highly dependent on her mother for care. Carol loved Hope in a way that was unlike any of her other children. She never blamed anyone for what happened to her child. Hope died before she reached the age of four. Carol felt that she never loved any of her children more than she did Hope.

Carol Christenson did not get pregnant again. Her family grew through her children's children. She and Hank never spoke about the injustice that she suffered. Kayla became a successful litigator. She continued to go to church with her family every Sunday. Always in her Sunday-best clothes. Dr. Penny Albertson learned that there were no absolutes in medicine. All information must be critically accessed. She would never take results of clinical laboratory tests for granted ever again.

*

Although clinical laboratory testing is highly automated today, occasional instrument malfunctions are unavoidable. A system of instrument checks and double checks in place in every clinical laboratory minimizes problems. There is also quality control testing whereby samples of known analyte concentration are tested each day to see if the lab gets the right answer. Some laboratories have tried to achieve a level of excellence known as Six Sigma, i.e., an error rate of only 3.4 occurrences per million test results. Some industries have achieved Six Sigma, such as commercial airlines in regard to the successful landing of planes. Because there is always some involvement with humans, however, the error rate can never be zero for any process. For the clinical laboratory, in particular, there are variances in biology that cannot be predicted and, therefore, prevent the removal of all error. Fortunately, unlike airplane landings, the vast majority of clinical laboratory errors have no significant consequences. Since most test results are normal, if there were an error, of say, specimen misidentification, it is likely that one "normal" result would be substituted for another. I greatly respected Carol Christenson's values regarding life and family. She knew who she was and what her place was in the world. I sometimes envied that simpler existence. No cell phones, no laptop computers, no Internet, no emails, no iPad, Face Book, or Twitter.

Missing Lights

****

Cecelia was a maid at a posh hotel downtown. She was reserved, quiet, and content with her position in life. Cecelia was pretty, however a birthmark on her forehead detracted somewhat from her looks. She tried to cover this spot by wearing her hair with bangs.

There was a rock and roll concert on Saturday night. The band chose Cecelia's hotel for their stay. They booked the entire penthouse of suites for band members and traveling staff. The band played to a packed house at the auditorium down the street from the hotel. Upon returning, band members partied heavily through the night. In their suite, there was a lot of alcohol, drugs, and girls who were invited to the room. These groupies were only looking for one thing. They all got what they were looking for that night. By eleven o'clock the next morning, most of the band members and their friends were awake and were downstairs eating breakfast.

Cecelia knocked onto the door of the penthouse suite. She knew there would be a mess and it would take her and the other maids several hours to completely clean the room. She knocked on the brass door knob with her key and shouted out "Maid." When she heard no response, she unlocked the door and entered. She started to straighten out the parlor room of the suite, thinking that nobody was present. She brought a large garbage bag and started to pick up the empty beer cans, and wine bottles, and emptied the ash trays full of cigarette butts and reefers. Then she heard a moan coming from the bedroom. Somebody was still there. She wasn't sure if she should leave or continue cleaning.

She re-announced her presence "Hello? The maid is here to clean." Johnnie Newman who was the band's keyboard player, came out dressed in a bathrobe. He was hung over from last night's frolicking. When he saw her, he was startled by her looks and was immediately attracted to her. From his drunken haze, he couldn't see Cecelia's birthmark. "Please stay and continue your work" he said as he sat down on the sofa to watch her clean. She was getting an uneasy feeling having someone watch her every move. She stayed because she thought one of the other maids would come in soon to help her clean. She didn't know that one of the other girls called in sick that morning and the maid staff was short-handed. After 10 minutes, Johnnie called for her to come in to tidy up the bedroom. When she entered, Johnnie was behind the door. He closed it behind him. With Cecelia sill in the room, he grabbed her. Cecelia tried to resist, but he was strong. He pushed her onto the bed face down and jumped on top of her. He lifted her skirt, opened his robe and raped her. Cecelia was crying quietly but did not shout. She was in shock as to what was happening. When he was done, he told her that if she said anything, he would deny it and have her fired from her job. Cecelia left the room and the hotel and ran home. She lived with her single mother in a small apartment near downtown. Her mother was working as a waitress at a nearby diner.

Cecelia never told anyone that she was raped. Within a few weeks, she learned that she was pregnant by the musician. The band moved on and was no longer in town. Cecelia's mom was surprised when she learned of Cecelia's pregnancy because Cecelia did not date a lot or have boyfriends. Cecelia did not reveal to her mother or anyone else who the father was because she was ashamed of what happened. She and her mother were not sure how they were going to care for the child, but an abortion was never a consideration. The two of them would just have to work harder to raise this child.

Cecelia's mom found an obstetrician, Dr. Robert Mendez. Cecelia was diligent in attending all of her prenatal appointments. Cecelia concealed her pregnancy from her employers, hoping to work as long as possible. She was successful in doing this because Cecelia did not gain much weight. Her apron hid her mildly protruding stomach from her bosses. The other maids knew but didn't say anything.

During her eighth month of pregnancy, Cecelia started

to have labor pains. She went to the General Hospital for care Dr. Mendez was called to see her. He was concerned that she might deliver too soon.

"Am I having my baby now?" Cecelia asked Dr. Mendez.

"Quite possibly" he said to her. "But we need to be certain that if we deliver your child now, it will be mature enough to breathe on his own." For many weeks, they knew that Cecelia was carrying a boy. "We are going to conduct a laboratory test that will help us determine this."

A long needle was inserted into Cecelia's abdomen and a few ounces of amniotic fluid were removed. Amniotic fluid surrounds the developing fetus to nourish it while in the womb. "We'll see if now is a good time for you to have this baby."

The amniotic fluid sample was sent to my laboratory for testing. Because Cecelia's contractions started early relative to her gestation, Dr. Mendez's was concerned that if the baby was born now, it might have difficulties breathing during the first days of life. Newborn lungs require a minimum concentration of a surfactant called "lecithin." A coating of this detergent-like substance helps maintain the integrity of the infant's lungs. Years ago, it would have taken my laboratory 4-5 hours to measure the ratio of lecithin or "L" to another surfactant, spingomyelin or "S" within amniotic fluid.

"Today, we can do this test in minutes" I told Melissa, my medical technology student who was present when the sample arrived into the laboratory. I was so happy to have stopped doing the L/S ratio test years ago because it took 5 hours to perform. "Surfactants self-aggregate into small particles called "lamellar bodies" that can be counted using our hematology instruments." My students knew that the hematology analyzer counts the number of red cells, white cells, and platelets from blood. "If the number of aggregates exceeds our threshold, we can tell Dr. Mendez that the baby is mature enough to be delivered," I explained while we were waiting for the result. A minute later, the lamellar count was 28,000.

"What does this mean?" my student asked.

"This result is just below our threshold of 35,000 which means that if this baby is delivered now, it may suffer from respiratory distress syndrome. This is a serious condition of prematurity that must be avoided if possible. Her doctor will have to give a drug that will delay labor for a few more days."

Cecelia was given an anti-labor medication which stopped her contractions and she was sent home. A week later, her labor pains returned and she went back to the hospital. This time, Dr. Mendez noticed a significant amount of fluid discharge from her vagina. "We will need to test this liquid to determine if it is amniotic fluid. If your 'water has broken' it is definitely time to deliver your child."

Cecelia's vagina was swabbed, a sample was put into a tube and sent to my laboratory for the fetal fibronectin test. A positive result would indicate leakage caused by rupture of the amniotic sac and that it was time for her to delivery her baby.

When the sample was received in the lab, we recognized the patient's name from the sample we received a few weeks earlier. This time, we were not concerned about respiratory distress syndrome because there was sufficient time for the child to produce the amount of surfactant needed to protect the lungs upon delivery, and a repeat lamellar body count was not ordered again. The fetal fibronectin test is performed on a strip that looks identical in appearance to a pregnancy test. Melissa, who was still rotating in my laboratory, watched the test being performed.

"Why are we doing another pregnancy test on this woman?" Melissa asked.

"The pregnancy test measures human choriogonodatropon, or hCG, a hormone that is increased during the first few weeks of pregnancy. Right now, we are testing for fibronectin. If positive, this result indicates that the patient is undergoing true labor." The test strip produced a line in the appropriate zone indicating the presence of this protein. "With this result, our patient can now have her baby."

The result was phoned in and Cecelia was sent to the labor and delivery ward. Within a few hours, Cecelia delivered a 6-pound baby boy. The baby was brown in color because Cecelia is Hispanic and the father was Caucasian. The APGAR scores were 8 after 1 minute and 9 after 5 minutes. The neonatology nurse gently spanked the child's feet which stimulated the child to breath and cry. At our hospital, we stopped spanking infants on their rumps many years ago.

Satisfied, Dr. Mendez said, "There was no problem with respiratory distress for this baby." He did a quick exam of Cecelia who was doing well and left the room to attend to his other deliveries. Cecelia named the baby Charles after her grandfather.

Although Charles was born several weeks prematurely, he appeared to be healthy. He had a birthmark on his arm. This was a coincidence as the formation of birthmarks is not thought to be hereditary. Birthmarks are caused by abnormal blood vessels from under the skin of the affected areas.

Usually with premature children, blood is taken and sent to my lab for bilirubin testing. Bilirubin is a breakdown product of hemoglobin that is normally metabolized by the liver and excreted. For children who are born early, the liver may not be fully developed, and a high bilirubin concentration can accumulate in the blood. Unattended, high bilirubin is toxic to the brain, and can cause a disease known as "kernicterus." Bilirubin exhibits a yellow-greenish color that can be evident when looking at an infant's skin. Children with high bilirubin are put under ultraviolet lamp. The wavelengths of these lights alters the molecular orientation of bilirubin to the extent that the infant's circulation can remove bilirubin more efficiently.

At my hospital, we were using a transcutaneous bilirubin instrument as an alternative to blood testing. This device measures the color directly through the skin and does not require taking blood. We validated this skin color test against our lab results and found reasonable but not perfect agreement.

Because Charles was half Hispanic, he had darker skin pigmentation than a Caucasian baby. As it is difficult to visually detect an abnormal color, the transcutaneous instrument is not as effective for detecting bilirubin on these infants. For this reason, the skin test was not performed on Charles. An order was placed for a serum bilirubin but the sample got lost and was never received by my lab. At that time, we didn't have an effective tracking system for specimens. Charles' bilirubin level was high and went undetected. He and Cecelia were sent home.

Within two days, Charles became lethargic, fussy, refused to feed and became irritable. Cecelia wanted to call the doctor, but her mother felt that this was natural for a newborn. Cecelia reluctantly put her child to bed but stayed in his room and kept a close watch. About 3 hours later, she noticed that the child was thrashing about the bed. Charles was having a seizure. She cried out to her mother to come. Something was terribly wrong so they called for an ambulance. Once at the hospital, the child was put on immediate life support. Blood was collected and we did a stat bilirubin test. Charles had a high level of 22 mg/dL. A call was placed to the blood bank for type O-negative blood. Charles underwent a double exchange transfusion in hopes of removing bilirubin. Unfortunately, this effort came too late. Charles became progressively unresponsive and died a few hours later. An autopsy was performed at my hospital and the cause of death was listed as "kernicterus." The high concentration of bilirubin was toxic to the Charles' brain. Melissa found out about Charles' death and asked me to explain a little more about how this could have happened.

"Kernicterus is a serious disease of the newborn and is caused by high bilirubin concentrations in neonates. Bilirubin is a breakdown product of hemoglobin. Most newborn infants have high bilirubin concentrations due to the rapid destruction of fetal red cells immediately after birth. Full-term infants have mature livers that can convert bilirubin into a form that can be readily excreted. High bilirubin levels are observed in premature infants due to the presence of immature livers resulting in a reduced capacity to metabolize the compound. There are also individuals who have a genetic predisposition towards high bilirubin levels. A variance in the enzyme UGT1A1 leads to reduce metabolism. Infants who have a variance in the gene for glucose-phosphate dehydrogenase (G-6-PD) can have an increased rate of red cell destruction due to exposures of environmental substances and toxins."

An autopsy was conducted on Charles. The pathologist wanted to know if there were any enzyme deficiencies in the child's blood. Samples were sent to my lab for analysis where we tested for both the UGT1A1 and G-6-PD variant. We confirmed that Cecelia's child carried mutations in both genes and he was therefore at very high risk for development of kernicterus.

After the autopsy, the baby was sent to the morgue where there was a private viewing. Only Cecelia, her mother, and a priest were in attendance. After the brief ceremony, Cecelia thought to herself, *"Johnnie Newman will never know that he fathered a child with me."*

*

The worldwide and US incidence of kernicterus are unknown because there are no registries available for documenting these cases. In Denmark, the incidence was reported to be 1 in 100,000 births. There has been considerable debate as to whether or not infants should be routinely screened for bilirubin concentrations shortly after their birth. The American Academy of Pediatrics stated that there are no randomized trials to demonstrate that universal screening and systematic follow-up will reduce the rate of kernicterus. Testing will not likely be cost effective given the rarity of this disease. The Academy is also concerned that broad-spectrum screening might lead to lowering the bilirubin concentration threshold for phototherapy. For now, the prevention of kernicterus requires careful examination by pediatricians and neonatology staff prior to discharging infants. Mothers and their families should also be aware of the dangers of hyperbilirubinemia, and carefully examine their children during the first days of life for signs and symptoms of kernicterus. An important indicator of jaundice is the color of a child's sclera. One that is yellow indicates the presence of excess bilirubin levels and a reason for immediate concern.

Premature infants have very low blood volumes, estimated to be about 100 milliliters per kilogram of weight. A premature infant can weight a kilogram or less. In an adult, 20-25 milliliters can be collected at one time for routine laboratory testing. But this volume taken from any infant, especially from premature ones, would be very harmful.

Therefore, every effort must be taken to minimize the amount of blood withdrawn to whatever is necessary. The use of the bilirubinometer can preserve the precious amount of blood available from a child. When not used or not available, the risks from not doing a bilirubin blood test greatly outweigh the risk from collecting a small volume of blood needed for the test.

Treatment of hyperbilirubinemia is more preventative than curative. For infants with an established diagnosis of kernicterus, a double blood transfusion is used where the child's blood volume is twice replaced with donor blood. O-negative blood is used instead of blood matched to the child's blood type in order to better remove unwanted antibodies.

Veteran Stones

****

Festus Bryant was sixteen years old when war broke out between the States. He lived with his family on a farm just outside Manchester, New Hampshire. Like other boys, he couldn't wait to enlist to fight against the Confederate States. It was a lot better than doing farm chores. But he was a little too young, so he told the army recruiter that he was 19. He grew out his little beard in order to look older. Festus enlisted and served in the 2nd New Hampshire Infantry Unit that was formed in early 1861, shortly after President Abraham Lincoln's call for 70,000 volunteers among the Northern States. The 900-man unit entered into the First Battle of Bull Run, near the town of Manassas, Virginia. Festus had never been south of Connecticut. Now he was a stone's throw from the nation's capital, which he had heard about all through school.

Although the 2nd New Hampshire fought for the North, they wore gray uniforms and refused to change to the Union blue. Because of the gray uniforms, there was some confusion between the Confederates and the New Hampshire unit. Festus was one of the men who was shot at by Union soldiers outside of his regiment. The musket ball hit his leg. While lying down, he called out to the soldiers, "Shoot the other way, damn it, we're on your side. We're from the 2nd New Hampshire." It was a flesh wound and Festus kept on fighting.

Colonel General Thomas Jackson, later to be nicknamed "Stonewall", led his Confederate troops to a decisive victory at Bull Run despite having a smaller army than the Union. This was largely because Union General Irwin McDowell didn't engage his entire army in the fight. Festus and his unit retreated to Washington D.C. Seven members of the 2nd New Hampshire died in that first battle. One of the deceased was Festus' neighbor from a farm less than a mile away from his. It was clear to Festus that this war was not going to go as easily as he or anyone had thought, and maybe he should not have enlisted. The regiment would fight in several other major Civil War Battles during the course of the war, including the Second Bull Run, Fredericksburg, and Gettysburg. By the end of the war in 1865, 178 men from the unit died of battle wounds and 172 others died of diseases, accidents, or from other causes while being prisoners of war.

Festus distinguished himself as a brave soldier. At the Battle of Gettysburg, he saved a group of his men who were pinned down by Confederate gunfire. He risked his own life to attack the rifleman. By then, at the ripe old age of 20, he was a crusty old veteran. Festus survived the war and returned home to his farm. His mother immediately noticed that his experiences in the war changed him. He was no longer the happy-go-lucky teenager that he was before he joined the service. Now, he had a much more serious demeanor. He also had bouts of depression. He struggled for the first few years after his return. His older brothers died in the war so he was the oldest son left in the family. When his father died five years later, Festus became the head of the household. Festus married Annie who grew up in a house nearby the Bryant farm. Festus had seen enough of the United States during the war and was happy to live with Annie on their farm for the rest of their days. They raised two sons, Justin and Matt. Festus planned to divide the farm up and give each boy half when they came of age.

One day, when he was in his early fifties, Festus developed severe abdominal pain. It was more painful than when he was shot in the leg during the war. He was always quite healthy but now he was shivering and shaking uncontrollably. Although Festus was Caucasian, his skin was heavily tanned and leathery, the result of having worked outside his entire life. But now it turned a yellowish shade. Festus did not notice the change in his appearance. He was not the type to look in mirrors. If his family or his farm hands saw a change, they didn't say anything. It wasn't until several weeks later that his wife realized that something was wrong with Festus. His sclera, or the white part of his eyes, were yellow. It was an eerie color that no one in the family had ever seen before. They did not know what was happening to Festus. His abdominal pain continued. Annie sent Justin into Manchester to fetch the town doctor. But she waited too long to send for him. The doctor was busy with other cases and couldn't come right away. By the time the doctor arrived the next day, Festus was gone.

Annie dressed Festus' body in his best Sunday clothes. The family buried him in a pine coffin atop a hill on their farm. Many New Hampshire 2nd Infantry Unit veterans came to pay their respects, though the number of solders still alive from that unit was dwindling. Festus' parents were also buried at that location. A stone was hand carved and placed at the head of the gravesite. Justin and Matt took over running the farm. It was there that they raised their children, and then their children's children carried on. Over the years, the town of Manchester grew and extended its municipal borders closer and closer to the Bryant farm.

*

Over the course of a century, the original Festus Bryant farm was divided into smaller and smaller farms and ranch properties. Bob Bryant, now in his early sixties, was a direct descendent of Festus. Bob lived with his wife Mellie in the farmhouse that Festus built, back in the 1870s. Over the years, it was modernized and expanded. His property contained 4 acres. The family graves were still part of his land. Growing up on the outskirts of Manchester, Bob was fascinated with history, particularly the Civil War, since his great grandfather Festus and great grand uncles fought in it. Bob owned replica uniforms, firearms, and swords of the 2nd New Hampshire Infantry. He would participate in Civil War re-enactments with other enthusiasts from the area and beyond. Bob was also the family historian. He prepared a chart that traced his ancestors dating back to Festus' parents. At a very young age, he was fascinated when his grandfather Matt Bryant told stories about Festus. But there was a mystery that bothered him for many years. Nobody really knew how Festus died. Stories passed down through the ages suggested that he died of some sort of liver disease. But he didn't drink alcohol and nobody back then got infectious hepatitis.

*

The Lexar Real Estate Development Company was eyeing some locations to develop their new shopping mall. It would cater to the well-to-do, and they owned contracts with Neiman Marcus, Tiffany, and Giorgio Armani among other upscale stores. J.R. Niles was one of the architects hired by Lexar. J.R. was in his thirties and worked on several other commercial properties in the past. He was a smooth talker and snappy dresser. But he came across to most as being genuine. He was not out to cheat anyone. He grew up in Manchester and was part of the community. He knew his group would offer a price that was significantly above market value. One of his jobs was to find a suitable location for the mall. J.R. studied the pattern of new residential home construction and areas that were acceptable for retail space. He presented his plan to the builders who liked the location he selected.

"It's ideal," J.R. said. "The taxes are modest, and it's within one mile of the interstate." The builders nodded in unison. J.R. continued, "We'll have to buy out some farms that are on the planned property. I've already begun negotiations, and most of the homeowners are willing to sell. The most difficult will be a Mr. Bob Bryant. He's retired and his family has lived on that property for over 150 years. But he and his wife don't have any children or heirs so it might be possible to buy his land for a reasonable sum."

The negotiations between J.R. Niles and Bob Bryant were arduous. It wasn't so much about the money, Bob acknowledged that their offer was more than fair. Bob was mostly concerned about what would happen to the remains of his ancestors who were buried on the property. There weren't any recent burials, both his grandfather and grand uncle were buried in a cemetery, not on his land. J.R. told Bob that the relocation of family remains would be done with a great deal of sanctity and respect. Since Festus and his brothers were war veterans, they could be reinterred into the cemetery that contained other New Hampshire Civil War soldiers. Bob and Mellie finally relented and sold their farm to the developers at a reasonable price, contingent on a plan for reburial of the remains of ancestral family members. They moved to a ranch house on the outskirts of town.

J.R. hired a group of archeologists to carefully dig up the graves of Bob Bryant's descendants and to preserve their contents. Dr. Pauline Lewis was a professor in the archeology department and headed the team of graduate students and technicians. The pine coffins and the bodies themselves had long disintegrated and only the bones remained. The tendons and cartilage also dissolved into the earth, so the skeletons were not intact. Individual bones were in line where the intact body was. The archeology team painstakingly cleared the earth where the bones stood. Bob Bryant watched the entire process with fascination. He asked Dr. Lewis a lot of questions about their techniques and purpose. She was used to such queries from other guests who attended excavations, so she patiently answered each of his questions. A photographic and video record was taken to capture every step. Bob took copious notes. The archeology team dug up Festus' remains after they completed excavating his relatives. When they finally cleared away most of the earth, the group paused. There were five little white stones found just below the rib cage bones. They were not like the other stones in and around the surrounding area. After photos were taken, the stones were carefully removed with forceps and placed into a specimen jar.

"What are they and what do they mean?" Bob asked Dr. Lewis.

"I'm not sure, but I think they came from Festus' body," she replied. "I have a colleague who can tell us for sure."

When she got back to her office, Dr. Lewis contacted me at the General Hospital. I had worked with her before, performing DNA analysis from prior excavations, and was pleased to help her again this time.

Dr. Lewis explained why they were excavating these graves and how the team found these stones in one of them. "I'm sending a sample of stones to you for analysis," she told me over the phone. "I'd like you to tell me what they are."

The stones arrived the next day along with a photo of where they were found in relation to the bones. I went into my research laboratory and prepared the reagents that were needed to solve this riddle. I thought this was an unusual teaching opportunity, so I asked one of my medical technology students, Tammy Bartlett, to tag along.

"We get kidney and bladder stones from patients all the time," I told Tammy. "These stones usually consist of uric acid, calcium oxalate, or ammonium magnesium phosphate. Determining the composition of these stones allows us to uncover the diseases that caused them."

"How do we test for kidney stones?" Tammy asked.

"Infrared spectroscopy." I said. "This type of light is used in heat lamps to keep food warm in restaurants and in bathrooms to keep people warm after a shower. When this light is shined onto a thin slice of these stones, it can produce a spectrum that is characteristic for the composition of a particular stone." I crushed one of the stones, formed the pieces into a potassium bromide pellet and loaded it in the infrared spectrometer.

"Hmmm," I said aloud. "The spectra from this stone doesn't match with any of the spectra from our library. This is not a kidney stone. The spectra suggest something else but I need to do another test to confirm this."

From the flammable cabinet I removed a solvent that was labeled "methyl *t*-butyl ether." Under a fume hood in the laboratory, I instructed Tammy to add the solvent to some of the stones I'd placed in a tube. I sealed the tube and put it into a 37 degree Centigrade water bath. The stones incubated with the solvent for a full three hours. When Tammy and I returned to the lab, most of the stones had dissolved. We took a small amount of the fluid mixture and added it to a plasma sample, which I then submitted to my clinical laboratory for testing.

"What are we testing for?" Tammy asked.

"The cholesterol content of the fluid," I told her.

Tammy was now even more confused. She knew that a high cholesterol level in the blood was bad, but she didn't know that it could form a stone in the human body. When the result came back from the lab, it showed that the sample contained substantially increased cholesterol content.

"This confirms it," I said to Tammy. "Gallstones form in patients with cholecystitis, or inflammation of the gall bladder. It's a common disorder that is usually asymptomatic. The stones themselves are called 'cholelithiasis.' Occasionally, they get to be the size of pebbles, such as these. When present they can cause pain and biliary obstruction. It's more common in obese and older people. It can be caused by eating greasy meals rich in cholesterol."

"But I like a greasy hamburger as much as the next kid," Tammy said.

"You don't have to worry so much, Tammy, as you're too young and thin for this right now. But there is a genetic link among those who form gall stones, so you might have to watch out if your parents ever passed a gallstone before."

I then went back to the office and called Dr. Lewis. "These stones are of human origin. Based on our chemical analysis, we determined that they are gallstones." I told her. "But why is it so important? It's really not an uncommon medical finding."

"The great-grandson still owns the property and was hoping that our excavation of Festus' grave could tell us how he died," she explained.

"Biliary obstruction as caused by a gallstone can produce jaundice due to the accumulation of bilirubin," I said. "Bilirubin is the natural breakdown product of hemoglobin. Decreased liver clearance of bilirubin, which is a yellow-pigmented chemical, can lead to jaundice. Death due to acute cholecystitis is rare today. But a hundred years ago, particularly in rural areas with poor medical care, such fatalities were more common. This was especially true if there was an infection that spread to the blood. I suspect that your Mr. Festus died of the liver disease caused by these stone."

"I'll explain your findings to Mr. Bryant," Dr. Lewis remarked.

"You might mention that gallstones can run in families," I advised. "Ask him if he's had any problems with stones. Maybe by excavating the dead, we found out some medical information that could help the living."

"I never thought about that," Dr. Lewis replied.

*

When the Manchester Historical Society heard that Festus Bryant's bones were being excavated and moved to a new location with other Civil War veterans, the Society organized a big celebration to mark the event. There was a reenactment, but this time, they recreated the specific heroic efforts of Festus and the 2nd New Hampshire Infantry. The men donned the gray uniforms just like the regiment wore during the war.

A year later, when the Lexar Mall opened, there was another ceremony that Bob and Mellie Bryant attended. A small marker was placed on the grounds at the exact location of Festus' and his family's burial site. An accompanying plaque described Festus Bryant's role in the Civil War. Most shoppers walk by the marker and plaque without noticing it, or giving it a second thought. But when Bob and Mellie walk by, they think of their former life on the farm, and all of his relatives that came before them.

*

Individuals who are at the highest risk for gallstones are pregnant women, especially those who use birth control pills or hormone replacement therapy. Other risk factors include being over 60 years old, having diabetes, or being obese. Losing weight too quickly also makes one susceptible to the passage of a stone. Mexicans, Scandinavians, and Native Americans have the greatest risk for gallstone production, approximately 1.5 times higher than other ethnic populations. Most stones pass without any problems. Someone who has frequent gallstone attacks can be treated by surgical removal of the gall bladder. Failure to remove a diseased gall bladder can be fatal. Gall bladder surgery was first performed in 1895 in London, right around the time that Festus got his disease.

Patients whose stones lodge in the common bile duct may also undergo surgery to have the stones removed. Non-surgical therapies include dissolution drugs such as ursodiol and chenodiol. The direct application of methyl tert-butyl ether to the stones, the same solvent that I used in my analysis, is currently an experimental treatment option.

Explosive Blood

****

Farhad was the son of a man who owned a carpet factory overseas. His father wanted his only son to go into the family business with him. But Farhad had a natural gift towards science and wanted something else for himself. Farhad went to a local college in their home country and got a Bachelor's degree in chemistry. He applied and got into graduate school at a major university in the U.S. Farhad was near the top of his class, and within two years, Farhad received a master's degree in organic chemistry. He excelled in the subspecialty of chemical synthesis and characterization. After graduation, Farhad set out to look for a job in America; the year was 2007. America was still reeling from the 9-11 attack by al Qaeda. Individuals from Arabic speaking countries were discriminated against when it came to getting high paying technical jobs. Farhad was granted several interviews and went on tours of their labs. But ultimately, he was denied employment by all of the companies he applied to. They all said the same thing, "You didn't have any prior work experience." But Farhad's American colleagues, who were less qualified than he, had no problems getting entry-level jobs. Being a foreigner, it was difficult for him to legally challenge these decisions on the grounds of job or racial discrimination. Despite his failures, Farhad wanted to stay in the U.S. To help out his son, Farhad's father opened an office to import his rugs and Farhad reluctantly agreed to be the operations manager. While this was not the reason he came to America, it was better than going home. It was also a means to get a work permit. He always hoped that eventually he would leave this job and work as a chemist. He knew he needed to keep up with the science so he regularly read articles from periodicals such as the Journal of the American Chemical Society.

Farhad's passion was soccer. He joined a local league and played games every weekend. He felt at home on the field as there were other Arab-speaking players on the teams. One game in particular was played on a very warm and humid afternoon. During the second half, Farhad became very fatigued and asked to be taken out of the game. He had a headache and became progressively dizzy as he sat on the bench. Within a few minutes, he passed out and fell backwards onto the ground. The game stopped and everyone rushed over to attend to him. The other players came and tried to give him water thinking that he was simply dehydrated. A wet towel was placed over his head. When he did not respond, a teammate called for an ambulance. Within a few minutes, the ambulance arrived and drove directly onto the field with lights a blazing. The put him onto a gurney and were soon off to the General Hospital.

The EMT made an advanced call to the emergency room. "We have a 20s something male who is unconscious and is having difficulty breathing. We are giving him oxygen. There does not appear to be trauma. His pupils are equal and reactive to light. His blood pressure is normal. His physical appearance is pale and he has cyanotic nail beds. There is a bluish hue to his skin. We have established an intravenous line."

The ER nurse who took the call knew what might be happening and prepared for Farhad's arrival. Once in the ER, Farhad was given more oxygen and an arterial line was inserted. An arterial blood sample was removed from the line via a syringe and sent to the laboratory. The sample was tested for blood gases, electrolytes, and co-oximetry. All of these parameters were normal except for the results of the co-oximeter. This is an instrument that determines the percent of a patient's hemoglobin that is saturated with oxygen. Normally the "O_2 saturation" is between 93 and 100%. Farhad's result was 74%. This test also measures the carboxy- and methemoglobin concentrations. Exposure to carbon monoxide such as a fire or from a faulty gas furnace will cause high carboxyhemoglobin levels but the results were normal in Farhad's blood. Instead, his 23% methemoglobin concentration was 15 times higher than the normal limit. He was treated with a strong reducing agent. Within an hour, his oxygen saturation was restored and the color returned to his face and skin. He was kept in the unit for overnight observation.

The next morning while Farhad was still asleep, the emergency department team was doing morning rounds near his bed. Dr. Sylvan Platt was the ED resident reciting the case from his notes to the attending doctors, other ED residents, and medical students.

"This patient has a diagnosis of methemoglobinemia, whereby the iron in his hemoglobin has been oxidized from the ferrous or plus 2 state to the ferric or plus 3 state. Methemoglobinemia has significantly reduced his ability to release oxygen to tissues."

One of the medical students who were present when Farhad first arrived in the ED asked about results from his pulse oximeter, a device that was put onto the tip of Farhad's index finger. "Dr. Platt, the patient's first pulse oximetry result was normal. How do you explain the discrepancy between the co-ox and pulse readings?"

Dr. Platt responded, "The pulse oximeter is used to measure oxygen saturation but does not detect the other atypical forms. When these other forms are present, the pulse oximetry readings are falsely high."

Using this as an opportunity for teaching the medical students, one of the attending physicians asked Sylvan to describe the causes for methemoglobinemia. An individual can be genetically predisposed to methemoglobinemia if they have a reduced activity of glucose-6-phosphate dehydrogenase in their red cells. These are important enzymes that regenerate hemoglobin back to the native state. Drugs such as nitrates used to treat heart disease, antibiotics used to treat infections, and chemicals such as nitrites, chlorates, and aniline dyes can also cause this oxygen desaturation. We have alerted the poison center, who will be here shortly for a consultation." Dr. Platt concluded his review and the team moved en mass to the next patient on the unit.

*

My laboratory at the General Hospital offers testing for glucose-6-phosphate dehydrogenase or G-6-PD. This was an appropriate test for Farhad because individuals of African, Middle Eastern, or Southeastern descent have the highest incidence of this disorder. Individuals with this enzyme deficiency can trigger a methemoglobin attack by eating certain foods such as fava beans. Farhad had normal levels of G-6-PD that excluded this as the cause of his problem. A portion of his blood was processed by my laboratory to be tested for methemoglobin reductase deficiency, another enzyme that can be a more rare cause of methemoglobinemia. Populations with a high incidence of this deficiency include Native American Indians of Alaskan or Inuit descent. Because this is not common among the patients we see at the General, we don't offer this test in our lab.

We were also asked to examine his blood and urine at the time of his admission for the presence of drugs and chemicals that can produce methemoglobinemia. A review of his prior medical records revealed that Farhad had not been prescribed any of the medications known to produce this disorder. He did admit to taking herbal medications but he was unable to provide the names of any of these products.

We performed several different tests to see if there were chemicals present that caused Farhad to have a high methemoglobin level. We used a simple "colorimetric assay" for the presence of nitrites. This involves adding a reagent to react with nitrites to produce a characteristic color. The test was negative. For the other chemicals, we used a liquid chromatography and untargeted mass spectrometry procedure. We identified the presence of amino nitrotoluene, an aniline dye and pigment. Given that Farhad was the manager of a company that makes rugs, the poison center sent an investigator to visit Farhad's company. If this was the cause of Farhad's illness, it was possible that others might be exposed by poor ventilation practices. Farhad resisted the idea because his company does not manufacturer the rugs themselves. But when it became an occupational health issue, Farhad was not allowed to refuse their request. The investigator came and after a few hours, confirmed that there were no aniline dyes found on the site. The cause of Farhad's methemoglobinemia remained unknown.

Dr. Morgan Perrone, one of the poison center fellows who were part of the consultation team was suspicious of Farhad's behavior. *He does not appear to be cooperating with us* she thought. *He may be hiding something.* Morgan had no evidence, it was just a feeling she had. So she took it upon herself to do some additional reading and investigation. Through an internet search, she learned that amino-nitrotoluene is a byproduct of trinitro-toluene, or dynamite. TNT breaks down into dinitro-toluene and under the actions of bacteria to amino-nitrotoluene. *Could Farhad have been exposed to explosives*, she wondered. Worse, was he making a bomb? She called the head of the poison center, and discussed this possibility with Dr. Tilden.

"If he is exposed to explosives, we need to notify the proper authorities. This might be a matter for Homeland Security" she said to Dr. Tilden.

"Are you saying this because of his ethnic origin? We have to be very careful that we are not racial profiling" Tilden said to her. "There is also the issue of our patient's private medical information. We can get into real trouble if we violate his personal rights."

"Isn't that for the FBI to decide? What if something DID happen and we had some advanced suspicions and didn't act on it" Sylvan pleaded.

"I will discuss this with the lab to get some idea as to the confidence of their findings" Dr. Tilden concluded.

*

Amino-nitrotoluene exists as a family of chemical isomers. These are compounds with the same molecular formula but differ in the positioning of various molecules. Toluenes are compounds with a hydroxyl group attached to a benzene ring. The other nitro and amino groups can be arranged differently within the benzene ring to form the various isomers. We found a high resolution molecular weight match for the compound but did not have a standard. One was ordered and the mass spectrum was obtained. When there was an exact match between the spectrum and the reference standard, we called the poison center and told them of our findings.

The case was discussed with the hospital's privacy officers. They concluded that it was appropriate to take this information to the authorities. The Homeland Security Office was called and the suspicions about Farhad were made known to them. It turned out they already had Farhad on their surveillance watch list, but now they had more evidence to act. They got a search warrant from a judge and assembled a team to enter Farhad's apartment. They covered all of the exits to his apartment building and then knocked on Farhad's door. One agent brought a battering ram in case that was needed. Through the door, Farhad asked who was there. When he saw the agents through his peep hole, he immediately ran out the back of his apartment. Agents broke down the door and the suspect was quickly apprehended. They forced him to the floor face first, and handcuffed his hand behind his back. Other FBI men searched his apartment. In a large locked closet, they found a "garage-like" mini-chemistry laboratory. It contained chemicals, powders, test tubes, pipes, flasks, solutions and compressed gas tanks. It was clear to the trained agents on the scene that he was making incendiaries in his apartment. Morgan Perrone was right; Farhad was planning something bad. Farhad was read his rights, arrested, and taken into federal custody. Yellow tape with the words "Police Line Do Not Cross" was strewn across the front door. Wthin minutes, the news media, having scanned police calls, were on the scene.

Upon interrogation at headquarters, Farhad revealed that he was planning on bombing one of the chemical plants who denied him employment. He was making a very small bomb and was going explode the device at night when there was no one working in the lab. He also knew from his job interview that none of night watchmen would be in the area to be harmed. With tears in his eyes, he told them he had no intention of killing anyone. He felt injustice and just wanted to make a statement. He also insisted that he was not a member of any terrorist organization and that he acted alone. The FBI did a search of his Farhad's computer hard drive, email correspondences, cell and land line phone records. They found no links to any accomplices. His father came to the U.S. to help his son. Homeland Security agents thoroughly questioned his father about his business practices but could find nothing nefarious. His father hired a high-priced lawyer. I appeared in court to give the toxicology evidence that led investigators to his apartment. During the trial, he looked directly at me. From his glance, I got the impression that he was out to get me. This is an occupational hazard that some people in my profession occasionally face. I have learned to be cautious but not overly concerned. Farhad was convicted of attempted terrorist activity and was sentenced.

Months later, I got a hand written package that was not labeled with a return address. Concerned, I did not open it and turned it over to Homeland Security. Behind a shield they opened the package. It contained a book that I ordered some time ago.

*

This fictitious case illustrates how a simple laboratory test was used to identify an individual with harmful intent. The production of amino nitrotoluene from TNT while chemically possible, is highly unlikely. In our real case of methemoglobinemia from aniline dye exposure, there was no call placed to federal authorities. The patient was not making an explosive device.

Shortly after the 911 attacks of U.S. citizens in 2001, President Bush passed the Patriot Act, extended for an additional 4 years by President Obama in 2011. This act enables law enforcement agencies with the authority to examine business and financial records, perform wiretaps, and conduct surveillance on individuals suspected of terroristic activities.

Beyond the Patriot Act, Homeland Security has publically stressed that terrorism must be combated with vigilance by all citizens. However, this does not extend to revealing personal medical information, which falls under the Health Insurance Portability and Accountability Act, or HIPAA, signed by President Clinton in 1996. Do the interests of a country as a whole have precedence over an individual's rights? What are the other consequences if an innocent person's medical information is revealed and is used against that person, e.g., insurance or employment advancement? These are difficult questions that should be addressed as medical informatics makes it more convenient for access and surveillance. We all know that emails can be searched and become part of public records. Can emails between doctors ultimately be disclosed in the interest of national safety? Farhad's rights were violated with the release of medical information to Homeland Security. However, the rights of individual citizens can be superseded in the interest of national security.

A Fib About Afib

****

Mrs. Barbie Ruggleman of Landmark Agency Realty first noticed that something was wrong with her heart when it beat rapidly and uncontrollably for no reason. These episodes were very uncomfortable and were occurring more and more often. A real estate agent for the past 25 years, Barbie now would sometimes experience these "tachycardia" attacks when she was showing houses to potential clients. She initially ignored these episodes and didn't seek medical help. But the attacks were becoming increasingly debilitating and were affecting her job performance. She was clearly a workaholic – the principal reason her husband divorced her five years ago. They never had children and she and Harry maintained separate incomes. It was an amicable breakup. Once free from Harry, Barbie could work even harder and devote even more time to making sales than before.

Now, though, at age 56, Barbie admitted that the long hours were perhaps taking a toll on her body. She typically loved doctors because they were rich and bought expensive houses from her. However, she dreaded the thought of seeing one for her health. But with her heart condition getting worse, she had no choice. So she made an appointment with her general practice physician, Dr. Joseph Rivers. Joe was a man of normal height with dark auburn hair. He was a wealthy man who came from a family of doctors. Barbie was immediately attracted to him the first time she laid eyes on him. On the day of her appointment, she was dressed to the nines. She was in full makeup with her fake lashes and blue eye shadow. The curls in her hair bounced effortlessly on her shoulders, and she made sure to wear her push-up bra so her figure would not go unnoticed. She wore a stunning Prada dress and Christian Louboutin heels, with a coordinated Louis Vuitton purse. At six feet, Barbie was already a tall woman, but her stiletto shoes added more to her height, and she towered over the smaller Dr. Rivers. She was determined to look her best when she saw him. Little did she know that all her efforts would go to waste. When she got into the office, Dr. Rivers' nurse asked that Barbie remove her clothes and shoes, and put on a standard-issue hospital gown. The type that has ties and opens at the back. The pale yellow gown, her least favorite color, was a little small for her and her fanny stuck out of the opening.

I'm not going to be selling any houses looking like this, she thought to herself. The nurse took Barbie's temperature and blood pressure, performed a 12-lead electrocardiogram, wrote down her height and weight, and transcribed her vitals into her chart. The nurse then left the room saying that the doctor would be in shortly. Barbie waited another 20 minutes before Dr. Rivers appeared.

I could never treat my clients this way, Barbie bemoaned. "*What makes the medical profession so special that the customers have to wait so long?*

When Dr. Rivers arrived, he asked Barbie the usual questions about her health.

"What brings you in today, Barbie?" Barbie described her occasional racing heart and the fatigue associated with it. Dr. Rivers then said, "Let's take a look and a listen, shall we?"

. *Hmmm, maybe he'll notice my breast augmentation and get interested in me as a person, not just as a slab of meat*, Barbie thought.

Dr. Rivers opened Barbie's gown and put his stethoscope to her chest, making no comment about her plastic surgery. She did see Dr. Rivers notice the tat on her shoulder that read, "Condo queen" but he said nothing about it to her. The head of the scope was cold and caught Barbie initially by surprise. The doctor asked her to take deep breaths repeatedly while listening to her heart. He then took her wrist and measured her pulse rate. Dr. Rivers' good looks were making her heart race and pound. He pulled out a small light and looked into her eyes. Her long fake lashes made it difficult for him to see her pupils completely. He went to pull on her earlobes to look inside her ear but her large Cartier diamond earrings got in the way, so she was asked to remove them.

"I'm never without earrings in public," she said to him, blushing slightly as she took them off. Dr. Rivers ignored the comment. He proceeded to look into one ear and then the other. He saw no problems.

"Your blood pressure and heart rate are normal," Dr. Rivers told Barbie. "Your cardiac rhythm is good as well, but these episodes of fast heartbeats are troubling. I suspect that you may have atrial fibrillation, or a-fib. This means that your heart beats fast and irregularly. I'm going to ask you to wear a Holter so we can be sure."

"Doctor, I'm flattered that you think I'd look good in a halter top, but do you really think that is appropriate for my job as a real estate agent?"

Dr. Rivers replied with a slight chuckle, "No, Barbie, a H-o-l-t-e-r" he spelled out slowly. "It's a continuous monitoring device for reading electrocardiograms. It is not clothing. Since your racing heart comes and goes, we need to be able to track your cardiac rhythm over time, so you'll have to wear this monitor for 48 hours. "

"Oh, I didn't understand," Barbie responded, feeling the blood rush to her face. Dr. Rivers escorted Barbie to the lab to be fitted with the latest Holter model. Five electrodes were taped to various parts of her chest and shoulders. The monitor itself was strapped to her belt. "This is going to cramp my style," she said to the technician, who ignored her comment.

When Dr. Rivers returned at the end of the procedure, he told Barbie, "Come back in two days and we'll find out what exactly is going on.

When Barbie returned two days later, the Holter device was removed. "I'm happy to get this off of me. I felt like a robot."

Dr. Rivers examined the computer printout in his office and returned to Barbie after a few minutes.

"Just as I expected, you have a-fib," he said.

A little upset, Barbie asked the doctor, "What causes this? Have I been a bad girl?" She put her hands on her hips and a pouted look on her face.

"Not at all," Dr. Rivers explained. "Many people get this because they have hypertension, or if they have heart surgery or have suffered a heart attack. It can also be common in older ..."

Barbie abruptly interrupted, "Careful where you're going with this, Doctor."

"In your case, we found that you have an overactive thyroid. Maybe that's why you are so slim."

"Dr. Rivers, I'll have you know that I do Pilates and the treadmill regularly!" Barbie said.

"Of course, I meant no offense, Ms. Ruggleman. I'm going to put you on a drug called warfarin. It is a blood thinner."

"But Doctor, you said I am already thin. Why do I have to be thinner?"

"No, I am not asking you to lose weight; this drug will dilute your blood. Patients who have a-fib are at risk for heart attacks and strokes due to blood clots. This drug will reduce these risks."

"So I'll take this for a few weeks and then I'll be cured?

"We can consider radio ablation therapy on you," said Dr. Rivers. "This involves precisely zapping parts of your heart with current to create scars, thereby redirecting some of the electrical impulses that are causing your fibrillation. But this technique doesn't work on all patients, so you may need to be on this drug or something similar for the rest of your life."

Barbie's eyes started to water, causing her makeup to slowly run down her cheek. She turned away from the doctor and wiped her face with hand. Her handkerchief was in her bag in the corner of the office.

"Not to worry Barbie, let's take this a step at a time," said Dr. Rivers, placing a comforting hand on her shoulder. "I'm prescribing you 5 mg of warfarin. You are to take it once per day. Eating green leafy vegetables also will affect your level of blood thinning, so please try to consistently eat a generous serving of these vegetables each day. You'll have to undergo a blood test regularly to see if you are in the correct dose range for the drug. A-fib is a serious problem, Barbie, because without this blood thinner, it can lead to heart attacks and stroke. But I'm going to take care of you. You have my promise."

With that, Barbie left the office. She was not going to let a-fib change her life. Since work was her life, she headed back to her office to review some new MLS house listings. On the way, she stopped at the drug store where her prescription was waiting. It was electronically ordered by Dr. Rivers' office. At the drug store, she also bought a pillbox that contained 7 slots; she loaded the box with one pill for each day of the week. She then took the first pill and headed off to work. She told herself she wasn't going to think about any of this anymore today.

Everything appeared to go well for Barbie during the first couple of weeks on the drug. She went into the lab the second week after starting the drug to have a "PT-INR" blood test, which determines the degree of thinning or anticoagulation in the blood. Dr. Rivers told her that she needed to have a result between 2 and 3. Anything above or below this limit might require a warfarin dose adjustment. Her result was 2.8, which was fine. The nurse said to Barbie, "Keep up the good work, and we'll see you in two weeks."

*

While PT-INR monitoring is essential to the success of warfarin therapy, there is new science underway that may reduce the dangers of using this drug. As part of my job, I've learned about the advancing field of personalized medicine, which involves providing laboratory tests that enable physicians to provide the right medication for the right patient, at the right time, and at the right dose. Despite these advances in medical science, errors – mostly mistakes about medication – continue to be a major cause of illness and death. Human error in calculating doses or in prescribing the wrong drug accounted for a small number of these illnesses or deaths. The vast majority are due to medical complications occurring in people who are predisposed to a drug's side effects.

While my lab was learning about personalized medicine, I was also helping to educate the next generation of physicians. "If by gene testing, we determine an individual is a slow metabolizer," I told the medical students taking my class in lab medicine, "the drugs will clear from the body slower than the average individual. Giving that person a standard dose may lead to toxic concentrations in the blood. Therefore, these patients should start out with a lower drug dose."

Johnny, one of my students, then asked, "Are there also some people who are fast metabolizers?"

"Yes," I responded. "These individuals break down the drug too fast, and they need higher dosages in order for the drug to work. The Food and Drug Administration approves drugs at dosages that are effective for the majority of a population. The problem is that giving everyone the same dose doesn't make sense considering that everyone is different. Pharmacogenomics is a new science that involves testing people's genetic makeup to determine their inherent metabolic capacity. This takes the guesswork out of drug dosing."

As an example, I explained about anticoagulants. "Warfarin is one of the drugs that are influenced by a person's genetic makeup. If you take too much warfarin, you are subject to bleeding. If you don't take enough, you may be at risk of a blood clot. There is a fine balance that is needed for the proper use of this drug. This is why the PT-INR test that you perform is so important to our practice."

Ever the inquisitive student, Johnny then asked, "Is there a way to determine who is a slow metabolizer and who is a fast metabolizer?"

I replied, "The key genes in warfarin metabolism are CYP2C9 and the vitamin K receptor enzyme. Individuals who have gene variances may be slow metabolizers and at risk for warfarin's toxic effects. In fact, last year, the FDA required to manufacturers of warfarin to re-label their product recommending that patients new to warfarin be tested for these genetic variances prior to being given the initial warfarin dose. We are hopeful that this will reduce the rate of bleeding and adverse events with this drug."

I convinced my hospital administrators that my lab needed to take the steps required to make these important pharmacogenomic tests available, even though it was going to be expensive.

*

After three weeks on warfarin, something terrible happened to Barbie. As she sat at her desk in the real estate office going over a contract for a pending condo sale, she felt dizzy and light-headed. The lamp in the office seemed to be exceptionally bright. Her temples ached and pounded at her brain. As she reached into her desk drawer for some Advil, she saw a bright white light, fell out of her seat onto the floor, and passed out. Her head hit the side of her desk with a thump. Her desk lamp was knocked over and crashed to the floor. The light bulb shattered. The secretary in the next office heard the noise and rushed in.

"Oh my God, Barbie, are you all right?" It was clear that Barbie was not all right. The left side of her face was drooping, and saliva was running down her chin. The secretary immediately called 9-1-1. The paramedics were in the office within minutes. They rushed Barbie to the emergency department. She was seizing en route, causing her body to shake uncontrollably. The emergency medical technicians did their best to ensure that she didn't hurt herself. Once at the General, the emergency room doctors did a quick examination and rushed her into the radiology suite for a head CAT scan. Their suspicions were correct. Barbie suffered a hemorrhagic stroke. Subsequent tests confirmed that she had a prolonged PT-INR test result. She was overdosed with warfarin, which caused her brain to bleed.

*

Barbie never regained her full mental and physical faculties after her stroke. Her medical disability forced her to retire from her real estate career and remain on medical care for the rest of her life. This once vibrant and sometimes extravagant person was now reduced to a nursing care-dependent woman who was medically much older than her chronological age. Her ex-husband Harry became the guardian of her estate and affairs. He consulted anti-coagulant experts who told him that warfarin was a difficult drug to control and that adverse events do occur at no fault to the doctors who prescribed them. Harry felt unsatisfied by this explanation. Out of love for his ex-wife, he started learning on his own about the dangers of warfarin and ran across some studies about personalized medicine and how some individuals were more susceptible than others to a standard warfarin drug dosage. He found one of my articles on warfarin and called me. He told me about his ex-wife's medical situation and wanted to know if we offered the pharmacogenomics test for warfarin.

"Yes, we can do the warfarin test," I told Harry. "The next time she goes in for PT-INR testing, ask them to collect extra blood in a lavender-top tube and send it to me."

Blood collection tubes are color-coded to ensure that they pre-contain the correct preservatives. My lab was just beginning to offer this pharmacogenomics test after some cost justification with the hospital. Only a few doctors at the General Hospital knew about it. Some of the cardiologists who were aware of it didn't order it because they felt they were so experienced with warfarin dosing that they didn't need any extra help, despite the fact that warfarin causes the highest rate of stroke in America. I knew it would be many years before the medical profession accepted this test as standard practice.

Barbie's blood was collected and sent to my lab, where my techs extracted the DNA from the blood and conducted single nucleotide polymorphism analysis, sometimes called a "SNP test". When the test was completed, I called Harry with the report.

"Barbie is a *2/*3 genotype for 2C9 and AA genotype for the vitamin K enzyme, indicating that she is warfarin-sensitive."

Harry responded, "English, doc. English."

"Oh of course, sorry" I said, "I'm used to talking to doctors. The amount of warfarin that was given to Barbie was more than her system could handle and as a result she bled into her brain and suffered a hemorrhagic stroke."

Armed with this information, Harry initiated a lawsuit against Dr. Rivers and his medical practice. He hired an attorney who had a doctorate in cell biology and was a research scientist before practicing law. An aide from the law firm found out about the FDA recommendations. Harry's attorney put the defendant on the witness stand during the medical malpractice trial.

"Dr. Rivers, we have genetic evidence that now shows that my client was a slow metabolizer. You prescribed 5 mg of warfarin, which was an overdose for her. The FDA has suggested in the relabeled package insert, and I quote, 'Lower initiation doses should be considered for patients with certain genetic variations in CYP2C9 and vitamin K reductase enzymes.' You choose to ignore this recommendation for genotyping and my client suffered a cerebrovascular accident. What do you have to say in your defense?"

At the advice of his lawyer, Dr. Rivers read a carefully prepared statement. "The recommendation made by the FDA is just that; only a recommendation. There are no clinical practice guidelines that have supported this view so far. In fact, the Centers for Medicare and Medicaid state that there is insufficient evidence to show that pharmacogenomics testing for warfarin improves outcomes. For this reason, they have denied reimbursement for this, except in the context of a clinical trial. Until there is more evidence, this testing is not indicated. Mrs. Ruggleman was not part of a clinical trial."

Dr. Rivers' testimony sufficiently compelled the jury to rule in favor of the defendants, despite feeling sympathetic towards Barbie. The court ruled that Dr. Rivers was not negligent in his 5 mg dosing prescription. Dr. Rivers felt vindicated.

In the hallway, Barbie walked up to Dr. Rivers. She looked very different from when she first came to see him months earlier. She was wearing no makeup or jewelry and her hair was back to its natural brunette color. Her eyes no longer sparkled. She looked tired and older. Her plain clothing looked ill-suited for this once vibrant woman.

She approached Dr. Rivers and uttered softly, "You said you were going to take care of me." She paused, scanning his eyes. "You lied to me."

Dr. Rivers felt awful. But before the doctor could come up with a response, Harry put his overcoat around Barbie's shoulders, and they walked past Dr. Rivers and left the courtroom together. Dr. Rivers turned to watch them leave the building. After a few minutes he sat down on a bench in the empty hallway and hung his head between his knees.

Barbie Ruggleman reunited with Harry, who never stopped loving her. Harry retired from his job and they moved to Scottsdale, Arizona. Barbie was better able to tolerate the warm weather. She was still on warfarin, but at a lower dose. This time, her drug was well controlled and she stayed within the target PT-INR. Nevertheless, she suffered a series of mini-strokes and died three years later. Barbie once told Harry that Dr. Rivers promised to take care of her disease. But it turned out to be a fib about a-fib.

*

The implementation of a pharmacogenomics test for warfarin has not become standard practice in the United States. However, a new oral anticoagulant medication, dabigatran, was approved by the FDA in October, 2010. This drug does not require use of PT-INR or pharmacogenomics testing for optimum dosing. The RE-LY Trial showed that dabigatran was safer than warfarin for patients who have atrial fibrillation. Time will tell if this more expensive drug will have a better safety profile than warfarin for patients who have other diseases requiring anticoagulation. In the meantime, warfarin will continue to be widely used despite its dangers.

Barbie Ruggleman's death was a tragedy that could have been avoided. Unfortunately, other cases like hers continue to quietly kill patients, since pharmacogenomics testing has not been implemented. In some cases, it is ignorance by clinicians regarding the advantages of such testing. In other cases, it is arrogance: "I have used warfarin for many years and I don't need an expensive lab test to start dosing," is something

I have heard from a number of my colleagues. I am hopeful that these attitudes will change with the next generation of physicians, who are increasingly embracing molecular analysis rather than dismissing it.

Lessphine

****

Nick Newman was a pharmacist who worked at a local drug store. Nick was very much a people person and greatly enjoyed his interactions with customers. He met his wife through work. Tess' mother was ailing and needed many prescriptions that Tess picked up regularly at the pharmacy. Nick was attracted to Tess the very first time she came into the store. He was careful, however, as there was a store policy against dating customers. Like doctors, pharmacists have health information on patients that require strict confidentiality. But he could tell that Tess also liked him, so he took a chance and asked her out. In order to not attract the attention of the other pharmacist, he slipped Tess a note while he was filling her next prescription for their first meeting: *Are you open to having coffee with me sometime? Signed, your friendly neighborhood druggist, Nick.*

Tess thought the note was cute. She said yes and arranged to meet Nick for lunch on his day off. Nick and Tess fell madly in love. They dated for a few months and then got married. One year later, they had a baby boy, followed by a baby girl two years later. Tess was working as a secretary at a law firm when they met. When their second child arrived, they agreed that it was better for her to be a stay-at-home mom. But now with only one income, their budget was tight.

Nick began looking at other job options that might provide a higher salary. He talked to one of his old college professors about opportunities within the pharmaceutical industry. He was told that because he was good with people, he would make a good sales representative. Through the help of his former mentor, Nick secured a few job interviews. With his intelligence and engaging personality, he did well at these interviews and received several job offers as a drug sales representative. It came down to a choice between a large company that sold a variety of medications and a small startup firm with only two FDA approved specialty drugs. If he joined the smaller company, his region would be larger, requiring more long distance trips and overnight stays. The larger company employed more sales reps so his territory would be smaller. He would have more day trips and could travel by car. Nick wanted to be home as much as possible to be with Tess and their two young children. So even though the salary was lower, Nick chose the job with the larger company, McDowell Pharmaceuticals.

Nick was assigned to represent McDowell's autoimmune drug line. He drove a minivan provided by the company to call on rheumatologists and immunologists to sell them their anti-inflammatory medications. Part of his job was to provide research articles describing the latest clinical trials using McDowell's drugs. He also arranged continuing education seminars that featured clinical experts from across the country to discuss novel therapeutic approaches.

One event was particularly important to Nick in terms of meeting his monthly sales quota. McDowell just received approval for a new drug, Osteba, for treating osteoarthritis. He planned an evening event at a golf country club for a fairly large clinical practice group that specialized in orthopedics and sports medicine. Not only were there a lot of physicians in this group, but they were also very influential in the practices of the other doctors in the area. So a successful continuing education program had the potential to produce significant future sales. Nick got permission from the regional sales manager to host the event. His manager was coming to gauge the success of the program and determine if it could be repeated elsewhere in the region. Nick was under pressure to make the program a success. He was lucky to have recruited Dr. Alan Toshman to speak at the event. Dr. Toshman was the lead author of a New England Journal of Medicine article where Osteba was shown to be superior to the standard medication in slowing the progression of osteoarthritis. Dr. Toshman's honorarium was $10,000, but Nick and McDowell Pharma thought he was worth it.

The night before the event, Nick developed a fever and cough. During the early part of the week, Tess warned Nick that he was working too hard on this project and he would get sick.

Nick didn't listen. While he was very accommodating of his clients, he would often be abrupt and short with his own wife, thinking he knew best. Unfortunately, this time she was right. His immune system was down because of his lack of sleep. But he couldn't afford to be absent for this event. He told Tess that he would take a few days off after the meeting. Being a former pharmacist, Nick kept a lot of over-the-counter and prescription medications at home. He went against the tenants of medical practice and self-medicated himself with codeine, which is more powerful than acetaminophen, aspirin, or ibuprofen as an analgesic and cold medication. He simply didn't have time to see a doctor and he wanted something that would act fast. So he took a standard dose of codeine and packed pills into his briefcase for his use throughout the day of his event. The codeine worked; he felt better and was ready for his meeting.

In the morning, Nick went to the airport to pick up his guest speaker. A Harvard professor, Dr. Toshman was flying in from Boston. Nick took Dr. Toshman to his hotel so that he could rest before his lecture later that evening. Nick then went to the event location and met with his assistant Kim, to make sure everything was in order. Kim got a perm that day and looked beautiful. Nick did not notice. Kim was finished setting up the registration area with badges for everyone who signed up for the meeting. Now she was erecting displays and arranging drug literature and reprints of key articles, including Dr. Toshman's papers. The dinner tables were nicely set. His guests would have their choice of steak, salmon, or chicken. A couple of hours before the event, Nick went to the hotel to pick up Dr. Toshman. He was eating dinner, so that he could lecture when the other doctors were eating. Everything was going according to plan.

Nick and Dr. Toshman arrived at the venue in time for the cocktail hour. Beer, wine, and hor d'oeuvres were served to the guests by the country club staff. Nick was pleased to see that Dr. Toshman was not drinking any alcohol since he was the evening's speaker. The room was abuzz with medical discussion among colleagues. Nick tried to listen in on some but also kept an eye on the clock to keep everything on schedule.

When it was time, Nick introduced his speaker and Dr. Toshman took the podium. His laser pointer was in his hand. The lecture was a success and Nick earned a lot of positive comments. Dr. Toshman minimized commercial bias by presenting both the pros and cons of Osteba. Several of the doctors said they would start prescribing Osteba for their patients.

After the question and answer session, the event was over. Nick was overjoyed. He said goodbye to his guests and drove Dr. Toshman back to his hotel for the evening. He asked Dr. Toshman to hail a cab to the airport for his return trip to Boston the next morning. Nick then got into his minivan and headed for home. He was exhausted and was looking forward for a few days of needed rest. But he got detained.

*

Beatrice Cready was an 81-year-old widow who lived in

the city. Her mind was still very sharp and she wanted to maintain her independence. So she lived alone in a 2-bedroom apartment. Her daughter and her family visited her regularly. Unfortunately, her eyesight was failing. When she failed the state's vision test, her driver's license was revoked. Every so often after dinner, she walked five blocks to her favorite coffee shop where she ordered a cappuccino. Beatrice liked to sit by the window and watch the pedestrians pass by. Lovers walked hand-in-hand. Kids zipped by on their scooters. Teenagers skillfully wove in between people on their skateboards or roller blades. Sometimes middle-aged businessmen in suits were escorted by pretty, young girls. Beatrice knew that these women were not their wives. They were either their secretaries or "ladies of the night."

One evening, Beatrice finished her coffee, paid her bill, and headed home about nine o'clock. The foot traffic thinned. She was standing alone at the edge of the curb waiting for the traffic light to turn red so she could cross the street. Suddenly, she saw a minivan speeding and swerving in her direction. She was terrified and was unable to move out of way. The bumper of the vehicle struck her in the hip, shattering it. Nick got out of the car and was horrified to see what happened. The police and an ambulance arrived at the scene within minutes. Beatrice was taken to the emergency department. She lived for a few agonizing days before dying of her injuries. Her daughter was by her side when she passed.

Nick was taken into police custody immediately after the accident. His van was impounded by the police. Once in the police station, he underwent a breath alcohol test. The result came out negative. While he had provided wine for his guests, he himself did not drink any alcohol. Nick explained to the police officer that he'd hosted a corporate event that evening and had just dropped off his guest speaker at his hotel. He said that he wasn't speeding. He simply didn't see Beatrice in the crosswalk. The officer then asked if he was taking any drugs.

Nick responded, "Yes, I have been taking cold medications." Knowing that cold medications can cause dizziness, the officer told Nick that they were going to collect blood and urine samples to be tested for drugs. He was then released by the police with the instructions that he not leave the area until further notice. Nick had no pending business trips; he just wanted to be home with his wife and kids.

A week later, the crime laboratory called Officer Huff to tell him of their findings. Mr. Newman tested positive for codeine. There were no other drugs present. Officer Huff remembered that Nick stated that he was on a cold medication. Nevertheless, he turned over all of the information to the District Attorney, Mr. Solomon Greenberg. Nick was charged with vehicular manslaughter. The DA tried to cut a deal with Nick and his lawyer, Brenden Collins, that involved an admission of guilt, but Nick refused the offer. In his mind, there was no willful intent or any negligence involved. His case was heard by a jury of his peers. The DA asked if Nick would be willing to be a witness and recount his side of the story to the jury. Being the defendant, he was not obligated to do so. Thinking that the truth would vindicate him, and against the advice of his attorney, he waived his Fifth Amendment Rights and took the stand.

"Mr. Newman, do you have a prescription for the codeine?" DA Greenberg asked.

"Well, no, I used to be a pharmacist and retained some of these pills for my family's personal use. I was sick the day before the accident and needed some medication," Nick stated.

"So you self-prescribed?"

"Yes, I did."

"Mr. Newman, are you addicted to opiates?"

"Absolutely not," Nick replied. "You can check my employer's record. I underwent a pre-employment drug test just prior to my starting the job. My urine was negative. I only used codeine for two days."

"Do you know that there are warnings about driving a car while on codeine?" DA Greenberg asked.

"Yes, but I was not impaired. I was in total control of my faculties."

"The lab told me that the amount of codeine found in your system was high," the DA continued. "They believe it impaired your judgment and caused the accident. Your car swerved outside of the traffic lane and hit poor Mrs. Cready. She is dead because of your negligent act."

Brenden Collins stood up in a hurry. "Objection," he said. "The DA is badgering this witness."

"Sustained," the judge ruled.

"I have no further questions of this witness," the DA concluded. The defense put up their case that it was just an unfortunate accident. They brought witnesses including Dr. Toshman and his assistant Kim who testified that Nick was not intoxicated and was in full control of his faculties. After closing arguments, the jury deliberated. Within a few hours, they returned with a verdict. Nick was convicted of second degree manslaughter.

Nick was shocked by this verdict. The fact that the codeine concentration was high and he didn't have a prescription for it swayed the decision against him. He was to serve five years in prison. McDowell Pharmaceuticals was forced to discharge Nick from his job. It would not look good for a sales representative from a pharmaceutical company to be taking prescription drugs without a doctor's script. He was sent to the state penitentiary. Tess visited him in prison frequently. She kept the kids away because they were too young to understand what was happening to their father.

During the next few months in prison, Nick read as much as he could about drug testing and the medical effects of opiate use. At the trial, the DA enlisted the services of an expert toxicologist who stated that the amount of codeine present in Nick's urine was higher than expected for therapeutic use and that Nick was very likely impaired. His negligence caused the accident and led to his conviction. Nick now asked his attorney to provide him the police lab's original toxicology results. When he received them, he saw that there was something amiss. The mass spectrometry results showed that while he did have a high codeine concentration, there was no morphine in either his blood or urine. Codeine is a prodrug that has to be converted to morphine by liver enzymes in order for it to exert its pharmacologic effects. Nick knew that he wasn't impaired by codeine but he couldn't prove it during the trial. The DA's expert stated that Nick was alert when the police arrived immediately after the accident because of an "adrenaline rush" from the collision itself. Now, it appeared that Nick had objective evidence that he was not impaired at all. He contacted his lawyer about the possibility of a new trial based on this information. .

I was called to help provide the new evidence for Nick's appeal. My laboratory regularly performed tests for opiates and I was involved with the interpretation of results. We also had tests that could be used to determine if Nick carried any genetic variances. After reviewing the documents, I told Nick's lawyer that there could be two reasons why the morphine level was low in Nick's blood. Either it was due to the presence of other drugs that inhibited Nick's liver to metabolize codeine, or he had a mutation in his genes that caused his liver to not produce the necessary metabolic enzymes. Nick was not taking any other drugs on the day of the accident, which was confirmed by the crime lab's toxicology report. So I suggested that they collect blood on Nick and have his DNA analyzed for genes that encode cytochrome P450 2D6.

"This gene encodes an enzyme that is responsible for the breakdown of codeine into morphine," I told Nick and Brenden in a meeting at the prison. "If we can show that you are a poor metabolizer, we can argue that you were not impaired and that the collision was just an accident."

Since needles for obtaining Nick's blood were not permitted into the conference room at the prison, I instead used specially marked cotton swabs and instructed Nick to scrape the inside of his cheeks. "The cells from your cheeks can be extracted for DNA, and from this we can determine if you are a slow metabolizer." Brenden and I left the penitentiary and I instructed my lab to test Nick's DNA. After a week, the result of the 2D6 test was completed, and I called Brenden with the news.

"Nick has a 2D6 *4/*4 genotype," I told him. "This genotype is associated with poor drug metabolism and explains why there was no morphine in Nick's blood. Codeine is a drug that simply does not work for him. At the same time, he doesn't suffer from any of its side effects. I believe we can petition the court for a new trial based on this information. In the last few years, the court has been very lenient in reopening cases with the introduction of new DNA evidence. This has resulted in some verdicts being overturned. But most of these cases related to DNA evidence, with the lack of a match excluding a person from a crime scene. In Nick's case, genetic information would factor into the interpretation of drug levels.

The appeal of Nick Newman's case was successful. A different district attorney reviewed the case and my deposition. Nick was still responsible for the death of Beatrice Cready, but it was not due to negligence. The DA offered a deal where the sentence was reduced to time already served. Nick was free to return to his home and family. He started over with a new job, but at least he was now out of prison.

Brenden told me that this was the first time that pharmacogenomics information was used in an appeal. He said that this is what makes the law so interesting because science brings new precedents.

In thinking about this case, I concluded something that only toxicologists could appreciate. Nick was getting "les-phine," meaning no conversion from codeine, and not "more-phine," the normal metabolite."

*

The cytochrome P450 2D6 protein is the liver enzyme responsible for metabolizing more therapeutic drugs than any of our other liver enzymes. In addition to the opiates, such as codeine, 2D6 also metabolizes anticonvulsants, antidepressants, and some cancer drugs. About 6-10% of the Caucasian population including Nick, are poor metabolizers for 2D6.

Some people are just the opposite: they are classified as "ultra-rapid metabolizers." These individuals have multiple copies of the 2D6 gene and produce more enzyme than normal. For prodrugs like codeine, individuals who are ultra-metabolizers will produce too much of the active drug. Women with the ultra-rapid metabolizing genotype who are breastfeeding and are taking codeine must be careful that they don't accidently overdose their child with morphine; fatalities have occurred. As such, the FDA has warned physicians and their patients about the dangers of using codeine.

Nick Newman learned his lesson the hard way. Self-prescription and medication by healthcare workers is discouraged because individuals cannot provide objective assessments of themselves. While they may think that they know best about their own bodies, such arrogance can lead to misdiagnoses and improper therapies. I am asked by my family members to professionally opine on the appropriateness of therapeutics. While I try to resist, I find myself caught in this web of temptation.

Easy access to prescription drugs can also lead to abuse of these medications, a particular problem for the pharmacy profession. Nick's use of an opiate medication without a prescription was illegal despite the fact that the drug was not being used for recreational purposes. When he went home, Nick discarded all the illegal drugs that were in his medicine cabinet.

Ibuprofen Preemption

****

Amanda Voss was a college student majoring in graphic arts at the local university. When she was a freshman, she went through sorority rush in hopes of finding a suitable house to pledge and live while attending school. Her older sister was a sorority girl and highly recommended the "Greek" life to her sister. Amanda pledged a sorority and beginning her sophomore year, she moved into the house on the outskirts of the campus. Amanda liked socializing and attending parties. She had lots of boyfriends, but none of them serious. She wanted to be free to fully enjoy college life. Like many of her sorority sisters, she partook in drinking beer and wine, but never in excess, or to the point where she might pass out. That was considered unbecoming behavior and heavily frowned upon by the house.

In the early fall of her junior year, the girls had an exchange with the corresponding sorority from the same chapter at a different school. Amanda and a dozen of her sorority sisters drove to the other college for an extended weekend. The two schools were playing each other in a rivalry football game. There was a highly anticipated party at the sorority house the Friday night before the game, and boys from neighboring fraternities were invited. There were several kegs of beer and cases of wine that were brought in and consumed throughout the night. The house hired a couple of bouncers to make sure there would be no trouble.

Amanda drank several glasses of red wine. She had good taste in wine and quickly recognized that the alcohol she was drinking was the cheapest stuff around. "Two-buck chuck" they called it. When the party was over, around 3:00 a.m., Amanda and the other girls from her house crashed on various couches. They slept through most of the next morning. When Amanda got up, she was experiencing the worse headache of her life. She thought it was probably from the wine.

"It was that rotgut I was drinking last night," she said to Ester, one of the girls from the host house who was up and about. "Do you have any aspirin?"

Ester went into the bathroom and came back with a bottle. "Here you go, Amanda. Take two of these. I hope you feel better. Some party, eh?" Without looking, Amanda put two of the pills into her mouth and swallowed with some bottled water. She crashed back onto the couch and slept for another two hours.

When Amanda awoke, she was feeling a little better but her head still throbbed. She asked Ester for some more aspirin.

"Take the rest of the bottle," Ester said. "Looks like

you're going to need it." Amanda took two more pills and put the bottle into her pocket. She then went outside for some fresh air. The aspirin seemed to help and she was feeling better. But Amanda knew that the visiting student's section of the stadium at the game would be very loud and rambunctious, so just before the game, she took the bottle out of her pocket to take another dose. This time, she looked at the label and noticed that it was ibuprofen not aspirin. She'd never taken this analgesic before. It was always aspirin or acetaminophen in the past. The small print said, "For temporary relief of minor headaches and muscle pain, Phoenix Pharmaceuticals." She took two more pills and didn't think anything more about it and went off to the game.

Amanda and the rest of the girls returned to their house that Sunday evening. It was fun but classes resumed on Monday. Amanda threw the ibuprofen bottle into her top drawer. Two weekends later, her house hosted a reunion for alumni who returned to campus to meet the current sisters to network and trade stories. There would various outdoor games and a picnic. Everybody was required to participate. Amanda chose the tug-of-war competition. It was five alumni holding one end of a long thick rope versus five current members holding the other end of the rope. There was a mud pit in the middle. It was a struggle, but Amanda's team, being younger, forced the alumni to slide through the mud. But before it was done, her team also ended up in the mud.

Amanda was sore all over when she woke up the next

day. She ached from muscles she didn't even know she had. *Next year, I'm doing badminton*, she said to herself. She went to her drawer and took two tablets of ibuprofen. The drug helped, but she still felt stiff. She took two more pills later in the day. By the next morning, Amanda was nauseous and had a fever. She also had a rash across her upper body, something she'd never had before. The sorority sisters drove Amanda to the General Hospital, where they did a work up for the rash. Dr. Royce Linden was an immunologist and dermatologist at the General. He asked Amanda some basic questions in order to determine the origin of the rash.

"Amanda, do you have any allergies that you know of?" asked Dr. Linden,

"No, nothing that Mom ever told me," Amanda responded.

"Have you been walking in highly wooded areas or uncultivated fields recently?"

"No, just at some picnics with the sorority."

"Have you been exposed to unusual chemicals, pesticides, or herbicides recently?"

"No, I am a computer graphics art major. No unusual exposures there."

"Have you taken any new medications that you hadn't been taking before?"

"As a matter of fact, yes."

"What drug?"

"Ibuprofen for headaches and body aches. I first took some two weeks ago and some more yesterday."

Dr. Linden was busy writing notes into Amanda's medical chart. After a few moments of silence, he said. "I think you might have suffered a delayed allergic reaction to this drug. It's extremely rare, but it can be very serious. We need to keep you here for observation and treat you immediately before it gets any worse."

"For how long? I have classes that I have to go to," said Amanda with a somewhat frantic look in her eyes.

"Depends on how serious your condition gets. Let's wait and see." Dr. Linden closed the chart and left the room. He spoke to the nurse about admitting her and providing her supportive care.

Amanda's health got worse. She developed a fever and the rash spread. Dr. Linden sent her to the intensive care unit, where they hooked her up to intravenous fluids. She developed skin lesions that the doctor covered with protective non-adhesive gauze. Unfortunately for Amanda Voss, the next three months were as horrible as any person could have experienced. Overnight, she went from a completely healthy, vibrant young woman to someone with multisystem organ failure. Her parents flew in to be with her. Dr. Linden told them that she'd developed Stevens Johnson Syndrome, a debilitating and life-threatening skin rash disease.

"How could this happen?" her father asked with a quiver

of fear in his voice

"It's a delayed hypersensitivity reaction," Dr. Linden explained. "During her initial ibuprofen exposure, some of her body's immune cells were 'sensitized' toward the drug and perceived it as a toxin. Think of it as sort of an army's 'call to duty.' During the initial attack, there may not be any 'trained soldiers' available to mount a response. But when the person is re-exposed to the drug, the patient's own T-cells are now ready to attack the foreign entity. Unfortunately, for some people, it also attacks normal, healthy tissue, including the skin, just like war has civilian causalities. I believe this is what is going on with Amanda and there is little we can do to stop it."

Blistering skin lesions covered more than 40 percent of Amanda's body surface area. Her health was deteriorating at an alarming rate. Dr. Linden downgraded her medical condition. She had "toxic epidermal necrolysis," the most serious form of Stevens Johnson Syndrome. When her kidneys failed, she was put on hemodialysis as a substitute for her own kidneys. She also developed severe liver failure and was put on the transplant list. Because of her young age and the absence of any other diseases, she was placed high on the priority list.

Fortunately, over the next couple of days, she appeared to slowly improve and the doctors were able to remove her from the liver transplant list. But her recovery was arduous and painful. Her sorority sisters visited her. Although they were shocked to see her in this condition, they were upbeat and cheerful with her. When they left the room, some of the girls were openly crying.

Eventually, the treatment took hold and her kidneys and liver recovered. After three months, she was discharged from the General Hospital and her parents took her home. She lost 20 pounds. She missed the remaining months of her junior year. She returned to school in the fall of the following year. She regained much of the weight she had lost, and looked like her old self again. The sorority hosted a big reunion for her.

*

Amanda's father consulted the law firm of Weston, Weston, & Johnson, LLC, to determine if there were sufficient grounds to file a lawsuit against Phoenix Pharmaceuticals, the manufacturer of the ibuprofen taken by his daughter. One of the partners, Harrison Weston III, met with Amanda's father, who showed pictures of his daughter during her most serious stage, and explained that the doctors believed it was the result of a single drug allergy. Weston assigned an intern at the neighboring law school to investigate further. The aide returned later in the week to discuss his findings with Weston.

"What did you discover?" Weston asked.

"Mr. Weston, ibuprofen was approved by the Food and Drug Administration as an over-the-counter analgesic in 1984. Since the original patent has expired, it has been available as a generic drug for many years. Phoenix Pharmaceutics is one of the generic manufacturers of the ibuprofen that Amanda Voss took.

In 1999, the FDA's Center for Drug Evaluation and Research noted that ibuprofen and other nonsteroidal anti-inflammatory drugs were associated with acute renal failure in several hundred cases, including several deaths. There have been other case reports that link ibuprofen use to severe kidney and liver disease. But neither of these potential toxicities is specifically listed on the ibuprofen warning labels."

"Can we prove that ibuprofen was the cause of Amanda's medical problems?" Weston queried.

"I spoke with a toxicologist at the General Hospital. He told me that there is a special laboratory test called the 'Lymphocyte Toxicity Assay,' or LTA. With a fresh blood sample, we can test Amanda's blood to determine if her cells have been sensitized toward ibuprofen. If we get a positive result from this test, it could provide a vital piece of evidence toward showing causation. "

With Harrison Weston's approval, the intern re-contacted me to arrange for blood to be collected from Amanda Voss.

"The test will be done in a Canadian lab. We have to be careful how blood is collected and processed. I will leave specific instructions with my phlebotomy staff," I explained to the attorneys. Amanda scheduled an appointment with my lab, where her blood was collected. The sample was sent by overnight courier to Toronto. After a few days, the result from the LTA came back indicating that Amanda tested positive for an acquired toxicologic predisposition toward ibuprofen.

Amanda's father and his attorney filed a civil lawsuit against Phoenix Pharmaceuticals for failing to warn the public and doctors about the hazards of ibuprofen. They were asking for damages for Amanda Voss' medical expenses and for her emotional pain and suffering. The plaintiff retained me to testify regarding the LTA and the effect of certain drugs on the development of Stevens Johnson Syndrome and Toxic Epidermal Necrolysis.

Two years after filing, the trial began. During a hearing with the judge, the defense attorney, Jeffrey Dempsey, asked me to justify my qualifications for testifying in this case and about the LTA test that was performed on Amanda's blood.

"My laboratory conducts testing for genetic tests that determine the genetic predisposition of Stevens Johnson Syndrome for patients taking drugs like abacavir and carbamazepine. Abacavir is used for patients with human immunodeficiency virus while epileptic patients use carbamazepine to control seizures. Individuals who have certain antigens in their blood cells are prone to developing Stevens Johnson Syndrome when using these drugs."

Dempsey did not completely understand what I was saying. To cover this ignorance, he proclaimed, "Your honor, this is not relevant to this case." He then asked, "Doctor, have you yourself seen any cases of ibuprofen-induced Stevens Johnson Syndrome?"

"No. Tens of millions of people take ibuprofen and there have been only a few cases of Stevens Johnson Syndrome resulting from it ever reported," I responded. "This is a very rare side effect."

"Then how can you be sure that it was ibuprofen that was the insulting agent?" Dempsey asked, somewhat excitedly.

I replied, "This patient's clinical history is consistent with the mechanism of delayed hypersensitivity reaction. She initially was exposed to ibuprofen and then upon re-challenge, her clinical manifestations began culminating with liver and renal failure."

"Could it be possible that she ate something or there was a pollutant in the air that day? How can you be sure?" Dempsey turned directly to the judge. "Where is the evidence that it was my client's ibuprofen that caused this illness?"

"Ibuprofen was the only drug that she was taking, and she had no unusual diet or chemical exposures. We also analyzed her blood using the lymphocyte toxicity assay testing. This is a test to determine if her cells have been immunized against the drug. The results showed that Amanda's cells were primed by a specific prior exposure to ibuprofen. It, or a metabolite of the drug, triggered an autoimmune reaction within her body, which then attacked her liver and kidneys. The lab tested thousands of other patients, and the vast majority showed no reaction to the test," I continued, while facing the jury members. I knew that these individuals needed to be educated about this test so that they could weigh the important evidence in order to make an informed verdict. I tried to talk in layman's terms, but it was somewhat difficult as I was used to speaking in scientific jargon to my colleagues.

"Doctor, do you do this test in your lab today to evaluate the risk of a patient?"

"No, unlike the blood tests that we do routinely at the General, the lymphocyte toxicity assay is only available in a specialty reference laboratory," I explained.

"Then how do we know it is reliable? Does it meet the standards for a clinical laboratory test? " Dempsey asked.

"No, this test is not validated under the Clinical Laboratory Improvement Act, which dictate standards for clinical laboratory testing. However there are dozens of research studies that have validated this test. The fact that it is not in regular use does not invalidate the results in this case. Scientific evidence in a courtroom does not need to meet clinical standards. It is my opinion that this, together with the clinical evidence disclosed in this case, allows me to conclude that more likely than not, the patient suffered an ibuprofen-induced allergic reaction." I was taught that in civil cases, there only needs to be a "preponderance of evidence," not absolute proof as in criminal cases.

The defense team acknowledged that ibuprofen was likely the causative agent in Amanda's illness, but in their closing argument, they took a different strategic tack. They emphasized that Phoenix Pharmaceuticals was not the original owner of the ibuprofen patent. The FDA granted Phoenix Pharmaceuticals approval of their drug under the Abbreviated New Drug Application, whereby a limited clinical study was performed to demonstrate therapeutic equivalence to the brand-named drug. There was no warning regarding the possibility of liver disease in the package insert of the brand-named drug.

Mr. Dempsey said to the court, "Since the wording for the instructions given by the manufacturer for the generic drug was identical, it was therefore compliant with the existing FDA warnings. Phoenix Pharmaceuticals is not obligated to exceed these admonishments. Such changes to the package insert require prior approval by the FDA. Since the FDA cannot be sued over its rulings, the district court could not preempt the federal rulings."

Mr. Dempsey further concluded that "over-warnings" can have a negative influence on the general public as to the safety of a product, thereby prejudicing my client's drug over the name brand or other generic drugs."

The jury agreed and summary judgment was awarded to the defendants. Harrison Weston told the Voss family that he would appeal the case to a higher court. In the meantime, Amanda finished college and took a job with a graphic arts firm. She did not suffer any further lingering effects of her illness. A warning sticker was placed on her driver's license regarding her allergy to ibuprofen stating that this drug should never be used on her.

*

All synthetic drugs have the capability of causing an allergic reaction. There are five types that have been described: Type I, an immediate antibody reaction to an allergen, such as hay fever; Type II, allergens create antibodies that recognize and destroy one's own cells. Type III, there is a self-limiting reaction to antiserum derived from a non-human source. Also called "serum sickness," it results in the formation of complexes. Type IV, a delayed hypersensitivity where the reaction takes place days after the initial insult, and after re-exposure; and Type V, an autoimmune allergy where antibodies attack normal tissues. The Type IV allergic reaction is what Amanda Voss suffered from. There are only a few laboratory tests that can predict whether or not a drug will cause a delayed hypersensitivity reaction. In the majority of cases, the development of an allergy is discovered after the drug has been taken and the allergy has occurred. The lymphocyte toxicity assay test can be used to determine if an individual has been sensitized to a particular drug and may be prone to a future adverse reaction. But the individual has to be exposed to the drug first.

In an unexpected turn of legal events, the appeal of the Voss vs. Phoenix Pharmaceuticals case was overturned by a higher court. This resulted from new decisions that concluded that federal law does not preempt state law when it applies to a "failure-to-warn" claim against a generic manufacturer of a drug. This court concluded that while the release of generic drugs was a means of providing more affordable medications to the public, the manufacturer was still liable for damages due to a failure to warn against toxicities, even if the brand-name drug was devoid of such a warning. The generic drug has the same degree of liability, not a lesser one, as the brand-name drug.

Amanda's cases showed me that all medications are potentially dangerous. While acetaminophen and aspirin overdoses have been well described, ibuprofen has had a much safer history. "While I believe that drugs are essential for the treatment of illness," I told my students, "we must always be diligent in prescribing them and be watchful for side effects. In order to minimize the possibility of a delayed hypersensitivity reaction, don't unnecessarily change the medications that you routinely use without a very good reason. If a drug is working, don't switch to an alternate one simply because it is cheaper. You may pay a much higher serious price."

Bottom up

****

The freshman level pharmacology class at our school of pharmacy has about 120 students each year. All students must attend the introductory class Pharm101, which contains lectures of the basic principles of pharmacology. Upon graduation, most of these students become pharmacists and work in drug stores filling out drug prescriptions. A few will go on to doctoral degrees in pharmacology or pharmaceutical sciences. Last year, I got a call asking me to meet with the course director of Pharm101, Dr. Carlos Esteban. He knew that my laboratory performed pharmacogenomic testing of patients at the General and wanted to ask for my help in teaching his students.

"Each year, I give lectures on pharmacogenomics and usually get blank stares from students" he said to me when we sat down in his office. Pharmacogenomics testing involves the analysis of an individual's DNA for genetic variances that affect how drugs are metabolized by the liver and excreted by the kidney. Pharmacogenomic testing can be used to identify individuals who are typical from those who are genetically variant.

Some individuals are inherently fast metabolizers while others are slow metabolizers. Because drug dosing schedules are based on individuals with a 'typical' rate of metabolism, an alteration in dosing will be necessary to achieve the desired pharmacologic effect and minimize side effects for those individuals who are not typical.

"I am looking to do something more innovative and exciting this year" he went on. "How can we make these lessons more memorable?" It appeared to me that he probably had the answer to his own question and either couldn't formulate it in his mind or wanted me to say it.

After a pause, I remarked, "Why don't we ask the students to volunteer for a pharmacogenomic experiment whereby we use them as guinea pigs?" I responded.

"What do you mean?" He asked. Maybe my gut feeling was wrong and he had something else entirely in mind, but I went ahead.

"Personalized medicine is about providing objective information in order to determine the best drug and dosage for an individual with a particular medical problem, right?" I said, then realizing that I was preaching to the choir. Carlos was one of the few physicians who fully understood the value of pharmacogenomics, and used it in his own medical practice and research studies.

I continued, "we will ask for volunteers to have their blood collected and genotyped for one of the genes that is important in clinical practice. Then when it comes time to lecture about it, we can disclose their genetic results from the individual volunteers to the entire class and openly discuss the medical relevance of these genotypes with regards to their future medical care" I explained, somewhat thinking out loud.

"But won't that violate their medical privacy? Couldn't this information have negative societal consequences?" Carlos asked.

"We must get this approved by our school's ethics' committee and have everyone sign a consent form granting permission to release this medical information. An individual can always back out of the disclosure at any time" I explained.

"There have been other universities who have genotyped individuals in the name of education, and have been heavily criticized by parents, administrators, and even by the media. Many students are reluctant to reveal their genetic makeup because it could cause job discrimination or result in higher health insurance rates later in their lives. " Carlos said. "How can we avoid this scrutiny?"

"The previous studies at Stanford University and the University of Iowa used a testing platform that revealed all genetic variances for the subjects examined. For example, mutation of the BRCA gene predisposes someone to cancer, apo E genotying to Alzheimer disease. I can see why this information must be kept private between patient and their care givers. The downfall of the exercises conducted at these schools is that they didn't mandate genetic counseling to students who had significant variances. This is a critical component when dealing with genetic diseases."

I went on: "We can be different if we focus only on genes that affect the pharmacology of medications. While drugs are linked to disease management, genetic variances for pharmacogenomic genes do not indicate that they will get the disease. It only affects the success of a particular drug to treat it. There is no stigma associated with someone with a penicillin allergy, and we can use another antibiotic." Again, nothing I was saying to Carlos was new to him. But he wanted me to think this idea through to its natural conclusion.

"I like this idea. I think it will grab their attention. I know I would be interested in participating if I was a student again. If you get approval from the ethics department, then we will try this for next semester" he said.

*

During the second semester, Carlos introduced me to the class and I told them about our plan. "I have phlebotomists standing by to collect your blood. You will have to first read and sign a consent form." Carlos and I decided that we would test each student for genetic variances to cytochrome P450 2C19.

"This is a liver enzyme that breaks down a number of different drugs such as proton pump inhibitors" I said. They already had the class on pump inhibitors which are used to treat ulcers. "None of you are old enough to have ulcers, but you will carry this genetic information for the rest of your lives, and it may be relevant to you many years from now when you need these medications or others that are affected by 2C19."

"In other words, when we get old like you and Dr. Esteban?" some student shouted out.

"Watch it kid" I said to the anonymous commenter.

I could sense that for many students, these comments hit a chord. Some of the others were seconds away from dozing off. Out of the entire class, about a quarter of the students signed up. Many of them said afterwards that they wanted to participate but couldn't stay over to have their blood collected. Some declined because they were afraid of needles.

Within a few weeks, we had the 2C19 genotype results for the participating students. We found that the frequency of variances from our class matched published reports. I incorporated the genotype data into my pharmacogenomics lecture that was scheduled the following week. When the time came, there was an eager anticipation for the results. The students who volunteered were particularly alert. However, even the other students were more attentive on this day. I gave the background part of the lecture first. I explained the concept of slow and fast metabolizers, told them what 2C19 was, and the medications that were affected by it. I focused on clopidogrel, a drug used to treat patients with cardiovascular disease. Some of the students got restless as they wanted me to reveal the genotypes of their classmates. Just before revealing the test results, I showed them an angiographic film clip of a patient with clogged arteries of the heart and who underwent an angioplasty procedure.

"The left anterior descending artery is 90% blocked in this patient" I explained pointing out the artery with my laser pointer. "Although he doesn't have any problems now, it is likely this artery will be completely occluded and the patient will suffer a heart attack." I continued to narrate as the film continued. "A balloon catheter is inserted into this artery and the catheter is inflated, and now removed. The dye is re-injected. You can see that the artery has opened up considerably." The film started again from the beginning as it was on a continuous loop so I turned it off. "A stainless steel stent was inserted into this artery to keep the vessel open. In order to prevent this artery from blocking in the near future, this patient was put on an anti-platelet drug called "clopidogrel." This drug needs to be metabolized by the liver in order for it to work."

The students knew that we all have two copies of genes inherited from each of our parents. "Studies have shown that patients who carry at least one copy of the poor metabolism gene for 2C19 will have a higher incidence of blockage in the near future because they are not getting enough of the active drug." Nearing the end of the lecture hour, it was time for me to reveal the genotypes for the student volunteers. I could sense that some students were thinking, "*Alright enough already. Let's get on with the genotypes!*"

The next slide gave them the information they were

waiting for. More than half of the students were "wildtype," that is, their rate of metabolism was "typical." The first names of the individual students were listed. When this slide was shown, there was some sighs of relief expressed by some of the students. A pair of them whose names were both on the slide turned and gave each other a "high-five" hand slap. "There are two students who are ultra-metabolizers. "A typical 75 mg clopidogrel dose for you will be too much for you" I told them.

Three students carried one copy of the slow metabolism gene. Looking directly at the students in question I stated, "Clopidogrel might not work for you and you may need a higher dosage or use of an alternative antiplatelet drug."

One student, Bobby, carried one copy of the slow metabolism gene and one copy of the ultra-rapid metabolizer gene. "We are not really sure how clopidogrel will work on you, because you are rare and there haven't been any studies on people with your genotype before" I said to Bobby. "It is likely that the fast and slow gene will cancel each other out but we cannot be certain."

"This last slide shows only one student that we tested who is a double homozygous for the slow metabolism gene" I told them. Freda Ng knew it was her because her name hadn't appeared on any of the other slides. "Freda, clopidogrel will not work for you." I made some concluding thoughts for my lecture, but Freda did not hear a word. Later, Dr. Esteban met with Freda to reassure her that she was not at risk for any disease as the result of this genotype. She understood and was not concerned.

*

That night, Freda was not sure what her emotions were when she learned her genotype and was the only one so afflicted. Should she be upset, angry, or indifferent? She got a small degree of friendly hazing from some of the other students at first. "Aren't you soooo special" one person said. "There goes the neighborhood!" said another. Freda knew they were just having fun and knew that nobody was really trying to ridicule her. *At least I know what this means, unlike Bobby, where the significance of his genotype is unknown* Freda thought. After a few weeks passed, Freda stopped thinking about this and went about the business of just being a college student at a large university.

*

After the semester ended, she want back home to her family in a small town near Chico California. A month later, her father, Horace developed tightness in his chest and went to see his family physician. Freda accompanied him to the doctor's office. Horace was 57, overweight, had high blood pressure and had a 25-year history of smoking until he quit a few years back. After a physical exam, the Doctor told Horace that he was going to administer an exercise stress test. He was hooked up to a series of electrodes all round his chest and back to record his electrocardiogram, and was asked to walk on a treadmill at a comfortable pace. Within a few minutes of starting, Horace developed chest pain. Several of the ECG leads showed an abnormality, and the exercise test was immediately halted. His doctor said he needed to undergo a cardiac catheterization and recommended Dr. Keith Logan, an interventional cardiologist in Chico. Freda remembered the angiogram clip that I showed her and the class a few months earlier. This memory now became relevant as her father was going to undergo this same procedure.

The catheterization was scheduled for a week later. Freda and her mother took Horace to the hospital where the procedure was to be performed. Freda asked Dr. Logan if she could watch the procedure from the cath lab viewing area where residents and fellows gather, but was told that it was against hospital policy.

"Family members can disrupt the procedure by asking too many questions at critical times during the catheterization. You wouldn't want your dad's test result affected by your presence?" Freda agreed. She and her mother sat patiently in the waiting room. Dr. Logan completed the test within 90 minutes and went to the waiting room to see the family. "The angiography went well. Horace has blockage in his major coronary arteries. We performed angioplasty and then put in two stainless steel stents to keep his arteries open. I am going to prescribe the drug clopidogrel, to ensure that they stay open. Do you have any questions?"

Freda replied, "Dr. Logan, I am in pharmacy school and we have read about clopidogrel. My father has a mutation in CYP2C19. Shouldn't he be put on an alternate anti-platelet medication?"

"I never ordered a 2E19 test on your father, how do you know he has a mutation?"

The fact that the doctor misstated the name of the test was not a good sign, Freda thought. "My DNA was genotyped and I am a homozygous mutant for 2C19, therefore at a minimum, my father must be a carrier for the variant allele. My mom must also be a carrier for the mutant 2C19 gene."

"Pharmacogenomic testing is not standard practice here. We follow standard protocols established by this hospital and medical practice. Dr. Logan was visibly annoyed that a 21-year girl was telling him how to manage his patient. "If there are no other questions, I have to see other patients." Actually, Dr. Logan was done for the day and was headed home.

Horace was placed on a standard loading dose for clopidogrel, given a prescription for the standard maintenance dose, and sent home. He was also asked to take aspirin each day. He recovered quickly and was back to work within a week. Freda returned to school that fall to begin her sophomore year. She stopped by my office one day to tell me what happened to her father. I told her that pharmacogenomic testing was still in its infancy and that many physicians have not adopted testing procedures.

"There are unanswered questions and concerns regarding pharmacogenomic testing. The testing is also much more expensive than a regular test. We have been largely unsuccessful in convincing all of our doctors to use pharmacogenomic testing. There are no national recommendations for its use so many physicians are taking a wait and see attitude. Because the 'top down' approach has not worked, we have taken a 'bottom up' approach."

"What do you mean by that?" Freda asked.

"By teaching medical and pharmacy students, the future healthcare providers, it is our hope that your generation will lead the pharmacogenomic revolution instead of it being driven by the current establishment" I told her.

"I hope this happens someday" Freda said.

"Me too" I replied.

One month later, I learned that Freda's dad died of a heart attack. One of his arteries had a complete block that resulted in a fatal arrhythmia. One can never know if this could have been prevented with use of the right antiplatelet drug. But it did appear to me that the top down approach failed for this patient.

*

Placement of a coronary artery stents is very effective in preventing heart attacks for individuals at high risk and or for those who have already suffered an attack. However, despite the advantages of coronary angioplasty and stent placement, a major complication is "restenosis" of the coronary artery. Angioplasty involves disrupting coronary artery plaques which can stimulate a blood clot and aggregation of platelets. For this reason, national and international cardiology guidelines have recommended the use of oral anti-platelet drugs to be given to patients after undergoing these procedures. There have been several clinical trials that showed that individuals who are carriers for the CYP2C19 slow metabolism gene are at increased risk for adverse events after cardiac catheterization. In the absence of an angioplasty procedure, there is no difference in the adverse event rates for patients with variant genes compared to wildtype. As such, there are no cardiology guidelines to date recommending routine testing for CYP 2C19. It cannot be proven that Horace died because of the wrong drug used. Patients suffer cardiac events even with adequate antiplatelet protection. In the absence of guidelines, Dr. Logan was not at fault for a failure of ordering this test or taking advantage of the genetic information that could be deduced from the genotype of his child.

The public is still wary of DNA testing for genetic diseases and cancer detection. In a recent survey conducted by the University of Utah's Huntsman Cancer Institute, 35% of respondents said they would not favor testing for genetic predisposition towards cancer, even if there was a positive history. Most felt that results would interfere with their ability to get insurance or employment advance, despite the passage of the Genetic Information Nondiscrimination Act, sponsored by the late Ted Kennedy and passed in 2008, that makes it illegal for genetic information to be used in this manner.

Moyamoya

****

Kazumi Nakamura came to the auditorium with high hopes. He signed in and got a name tag and number, which he pinned to the front of his shirt. For his entire life, he was told by his family that he had a wonderful singing voice. Now he had an opportunity to prove it. He was among ten thousand other teenagers and young adults, all of whom had the same goal: to be the next *America's Talent!* As a Japanese-American, Kazumi instantly gained attention from the show's producers. They asked about his life. His father was from Kyoto, where he'd met Kazumi's mother, an American, who was in Japan teaching English. Because Kazumi was of mixed race, he didn't fit in well in the grammar school he attended when he lived in Japan. Things weren't much better when the family moved to the U.S. There weren't many Asians in the heartland of America. As a result, Kazumi was very shy throughout his early years. Being an only child made his transition even more difficult.

When he sang, Kazumi was in a totally different world. His normal speaking tone was quiet and reserved, but his singing voice was bold and confident. He could hit the high and low notes equally well. He had a sense of timing with both the harmony and melody of a song. He was now nineteen. And he could be a star.

Backstage and off camera, Bryan, the host of *American Talent!* asked Kazumi if he was nervous. Kazumi was so shy that he could barely speak and couldn't look directly at Bryan's face. Bryan thought to himself, *this kid has no chance.* When Kazumi walked into the audition room, he could sense that the judges also saw his insecurity.

I made a mistake coming here, he said to himself. *They are going to hate me.*

Celia Lopez spoke up first. "What's your name, honey?" Kazumi thought that Celia was the most beautiful person he'd ever seen, which didn't help his confidence. He mumbled his name.

Andy Johnson tried to put him at ease. "Don't worry, dog, you're among friends. What're you going to sing for us tonight?"

Kazumi said, "*Isn't She Lovely*, by Stevie Wonder."

Vincent Taylor thought, *not* that *song again.* "Let's hear it," he said to Kazumi.

At first, Kazumi's voice cracked with nervousness. But when he got to the line, "But isn't she lovely made from love," his voice started to soar. He was a different person. He sang directly to Celia. He could see that they all loved his rendition. The three judges were swaying side to side in unison with the song.

When he finished, Celia held out her bare arms to show Andy and Vincent that she had goose bumps. Kazumi, being a regular viewer of the show on TV, knew that this was a good sign. Andy said, "Dude, that was over the top. I don't think we need to discuss this. Let's just vote. Vincent?"

"I say yes."

"Celia?"

"A thousand percent yes from me."

After a brief pause, Andy pointed to Kazumi and shouted. "You're going to the Big Apple!"

Someone from the show handed him a yellow paper signifying that he passed the audition. Kazumi rushed outside to meet his family. He almost tripped and fell. He was never before so excited. He was going to sing on *American Talent!*

Being selected to sing on the show changed Kazumi's life. His confidence soared. When the kids at school heard the news, he became somewhat of a celebrity. While he didn't have a lot of friends before, now everyone wanted to know him. He became friends with two boys in particular, Melvin Ostrow and Dean Terrault. Melvin and Dean were very popular with the girls and Kazumi wanted to be a part of that. After a month of friendship, Melvin invited Kazumi to accompany him and Dean for a weekend ski trip. Melvin's family owned a lodge. Kazumi had never skied before so he took lessons. After a long hard day of skiing, they all settled down in the cabin for the evening.

Kazumi ordered pizza for delivery. Melvin brought Heineken beer. Dean brought designer amines.

"Don't worry," he said to his friends. "I synthesized these in my garage last week from a recipe I found on the Internet. I purified this batch to make sure it was clean."

"What are designer amines?" Kazumi asked.

Dean said, "They're hallucinogens like Ecstasy. The stuff I made is called 2C-I. I tried some of this in a club in London last summer when I was away for our study abroad program. It really expanded my horizons, if you know what I mean." Kazumi was reluctant to try it but Dean and Melvin jumped right in. Within a few minutes, they were both high. They appeared to be having a good time, with no side effects.

Melvin said to Kazumi, "You gotta try this stuff, man."

"You don't have to worry about coming down while on this stuff, like you do with Ecstasy," Dean said. So against his better judgment, Kazumi popped a couple of the homemade capsules into his mouth and swallowed.

Later that night after all were asleep, Kazumi woke up with a terrible headache. He had a history of migraines and sometimes got them when he was at high altitudes. So he didn't think much of it. He rummaged in his bag for some ibuprofen, swallowed two pills, and tried to go back to sleep. But the drug didn't help. In fact, over the next 30 minutes, his headache got worse. He turned the light on in the room. Melvin, who was sharing the room with Kazumi, was still fast asleep and didn't wake up. Part of the reason was because Melvin was drunk and had passed out. He was still in his ski pants. Kazumi realized that he couldn't see out of his left eye. When he got up to go to the bathroom, he became dizzy, lost his balance, and fell back onto the bed. His left arm was tingling as if it was asleep. But he couldn't shake his arm enough to get the blood flowing back through it. He sensed that this was more serious than just a migraine.

Kazumi shouted out. "Melvin! Melvin! I need help. There's something wrong with me." But Melvin did not move. He was still out cold. Kazumi shouted out to Dean who was asleep on the couch in the next room. Dean awoke, heard the commotion, and came right in.

"What's going on? Kazumi, are you all right?"

Kazumi spoke very slowly and in incomplete sentences. "No. Don't think so. Call, ah, ambulance. Need, need to get hospital." And then, he fell back and passed out on the bed.

Dean pulled out his cell phone but there was no service. He then realized that they were in the mountains. So he found the landline and dialed the operator. It took over an hour for the ambulance to arrive at the ski lodge. Fresh snow had fallen that night and the travel conditions were poor. Eventually, Kazumi was put on a gurney and he, along with Dean and Melvin who was now awake, were on their way to the emergency department.

*

Dr. Bernadette Berkowitz was the emergency department

resident on duty that night. Baylor Willerton, a fourth-year medical student was also on the floor. It was a quiet evening; only a few skiers were admitted earlier that evening with fractured bones. The mountains had not received a lot of snow that winter, and the conditions were icy. This usually led to faster speeds and more crashes by skiers. Bernadette was an avid snowboarder and was experienced with these types of skiing injuries. Kazumi was brought into the ED and taken to an examination room. A nurse entered and began taking his vital signs. Before going in to see Kazumi, Dr. Berkowitz interviewed Dean and Melvin in a room off to the side.

Dr. Berkowitz asked Dean and Melvin, "What did Kazumi complain of this evening?"

Melvin said, "We'd just returned from skiing. After dinner, he said he was tired and went to bed early, around nine. Dean and I stayed up to watch a movie and turned in around midnight. Later, he woke us up because of a bad headache that wouldn't go away, so we called for help.

"Was Kazumi wearing a helmet?"

Dean said, "No helmet, but he's a beginner so he was mostly on flat ground."

Dr. Berkowitz looked at Baylor and shook her head. She had seen far too many head injury cases that could have been avoided by this simple precaution. She turned back to Melvin and Dean and asked, "Did Kazumi have any bad falls where he might have hit his head?"

Dean said, "He was taking lessons. Melvin and I weren't with him, so we don't really know, but he didn't say anything about a bad wipeout."

Dr. Berkowitz wanted more clarification. "Did he do any skiing through the woods? Maybe he hit a tree and neither of you saw it?"

Melvin spoke up. "No, he never made it off the bunny slope."

Dr. Berkowitz asked, "Did he complain of any headaches or muscle pains before you went to bed?"

"No," Melvin responded.

Baylor, wanting to make an impression on his resident asked, "Were you guys drinking tonight or using drugs?"

Dean, the chemist not wanting to incriminate himself, said, "Sure, we drank some beers, but no drugs." Dean knew they were going to do drug and alcohol testing on Kazumi as a matter of routine ED investigations. But he also knew that the designer drugs they all took wouldn't come up positive on their usual urine drug screen. Melvin, staring at the floor, said nothing.

Satisfied with these answers, Dr. Berkowitz left the room to examine Kazumi. When both Dr. Berkowitz and Baylor were gone and the two college students were alone in the room, Melvin asked Dean, "Why didn't you tell them that Kazumi took the designer drug that you made in your lab? That might have an impact on his treatment. He may be seriously hurt. If you don't tell them, then I'm going to."

Dean said, "Relax. Kazumi told me that he often gets these headaches when he's at a high altitude. Maybe he doesn't get enough oxygen. I'm sure he'll be fine." Dean then pointed to their friend, who they could see through the glass window, lying in bed. "See, he's getting oxygen right now. Let's see how it goes. If it's more serious than that, I promise that I'll come clean."

"You'd better. Kazumi is our friend and I don't want anything bad to happen to him."

*

Dr. Berkowitz was conducting a thorough exam on Kazumi. She questioned him about the events of the day, but Kazumi was in and out of consciousness. When he was awake, he was dazed and confused and was not able to give completely coherent answers. His face showed signs of drooping on the left side.

"Head hurts. Head hurts," Kazumi said repeatedly.

Despite what his friends said, Dr. Berkowitz suspected that Kazumi suffered traumatic brain injury. She called radiology and ordered a head CT scan stat. While she was waiting for the scanner to arrive, she looked into his eyes with a funduscope. She was looking for swelling of the optic disk, a sign of increased intracranial pressure. She found no abnormality.

When the CT scan came back, the radiology tech, Kathy Carlson, paged Dr. Berkowitz. Kathy was new to the job, having graduated from radiology technology school six months earlier.

But neither she nor Dr. Berkowitz had ever seen a head scan that looked like this. Dr. Berkowitz sat back for a second, staring at the image. She then went to the phone and placed a call to the radiologist on call for the evening.

Dr. David Zhang was in bed when the call came. He always had the phone by his bed so that when it rang, he could get it quickly, minimizing any disturbance to his wife. He grabbed the phone after one ring.

"Dr. Zhang, this is Dr. Berkowitz at Sierra Hospital. I'm sorry to bother you at this hour," she looked at her watch and noted that it was 2:00 a.m., "but I have an unusual head CT image and I need your help. This is a 19-year old with a chief complaint of headache. He presents with..."

"Whoa," Dr. Zhang interrupted. "Wait one minute. Let me get my wits about me. I need to get on the computer and bring up the image." As he was walking to his office in his pajamas, he couldn't help thinking that his radiology practice group should have signed the contract with Brisbane Radiology Associates in Australia, who could field these late night calls rather than waking up the partners. Dr. Zhang turned his monitor on, logged in, and within 30 seconds, Kazumi's CT images appeared on his high-resolution 35-inch computer monitor. *In the days before tele-radiology, my life was much simpler*, he thought to himself. When he saw the images, he knew exactly what Dr. Berkowitz's concern was about.

"Your patient has Moyamoya disease. It is a congenital

abnormality of the brain's main blood vessels, especially the internal carotid arteries, the main vessels that feed blood to the brain. In this case, these vessels are considerably narrower than those of a normal person."

Baylor, the medical student, jumped in. "This is so different from anything else I've ever seen in class or in the textbooks. Can you describe it a bit more for me?"

Dr. Zhang continued. "Imagine two cities: a modern one, and an ancient one. In the modern city, there are interstate highways with many large lanes capable of carrying lots of traffic. In addition, there are other major roads that crisscross the city. Then you have the individual streets and finally alleys and back roads. Now compare that to the roads of an ancient city, like Athens. There were no major highways during those times; they didn't have trucks or a need for wide roads. All of the houses were close together, with lots of small streets and back alleys. Moyamoya disease is like having streets like ancient Greece."

"So if there is a road blockage in a large, modern city, cars can get around it," Baylor said.

"Right," Dr. Zhang replied. "But if a blockage occurs on a street of an ancient city, there is no other way to go. Or, in this case, there is blockage of blood flow to large areas of the brain, resulting in damage."

"But why are there so many tiny vessels in and around the carotids?" Baylor asked.

"Ah, these are collateral arteries that form as a

compensatory mechanism to the narrowed main artery. Without these, your patient would not have sufficient blood to meet the normal blood needs of his brain. From this CT scan, I can see that there is a considerable amount of blood in this brain. Your patient suffered a hemorrhagic stroke. Patients with Moyamoya disease have a high incidence of this problem."

"That would be consistent with his clinical presentation of unilateral weakness, headache, incoherence and slurred speech," Dr. Berkowitz said.

"What was the patient doing this afternoon and evening?"

Dr. Berkowitz recounted the conversation with Kazumi's friends about skiing but not having suffered a head injury.

Dr. Zhang said, "I'm not a neurologist, but he actually is a little young to have suffered a stroke, even in the context of the Moyamoya disease. Did the patient take any drugs?"

"His friends denied any drug use," Dr. Berkowitz said, "but based on this discussion, I will order blood alcohol and urine tox screens."

"Good luck," Dr. Zhang said. "Call me if you need any more help, but please wait until morning." He hung up the phone and slipped back into bed. Within minutes, he was asleep. His wife slept quietly next to him, completely unaware of the phone call. Over the years, she trained herself to ignore these interruptions of sleep.

*

A few hours later, Kazumi's blood alcohol results came back at 40 mg/dL or 0.04%, showing that he'd been drinking, but not heavily. The urine drug screen was negative for all drugs, including cocaine and amphetamines. These drugs are linked to vasoconstriction and may precipitate a stroke. Dr. Berkowitz was not satisfied with these results. There was something about Melvin's behavior that didn't sit right with her. He wouldn't look her in the eyes, and instead sort of shrugged his shoulders and mumbled, like he was hiding something. Dr. Berkowitz waited until morning and called the lab to speak with the pathologist in charge of the clinical laboratory.

"We don't have any sophisticated testing beyond the usual drug screen," the pathologist told her. "But there is a toxicologist at the General Hospital who has published on detection methods for novel drugs. We can send some of your patient's blood and urine samples to them so they can test for the presence of designer amines."

The lab packed Kazumi's blood samples and sent them by taxi to the General Hospital, where they arrived later that morning. Dr. Berkowitz called to tell me of her suspicions.

"I suspect that there were some drugs involved that may have precipitated the stroke," she explained. "How can you help us?"

I responded, "These college kids are very clever today. They can synthesize drugs from formulas listed on the Web. As a toxicologist, I'm finding it increasingly difficult to keep up with the new chemicals being produced. But we have some novel mass spectrometry equipment that might help. Give us a few hours and we'll get back to you if we find something."

I instructed my lab tech to extract the sample and inject it into the mass spectrometer. Almost immediately, a peak appeared in both the serum and urine. It didn't match any of our standards. But based on the mass spectrometry fragmentation pattern, it looked like an illicit amine. I called Dr. Berkowitz, who was still on the service after 24 hours straight, to tell her of our findings.

"I think you need to have a discussion with your patient's friends again about their possible drug use. Tell them that we have some evidence of a designer amine in the patient's blood and if they want to help him, they should come clean."

Kazumi was admitted to the intensive care unit of Sierra Hospital. Armed with her new knowledge, Dr. Berkowitz confronted Melvin and Dean, who were sitting in the nearby lounge.

"You boys need to come clean," she told them. "I'm not interested in incriminating you two, just tell me what happened last night so we can help your friend. You do care about him, don't you? My toxicologist thinks that Kazumi took some designer amines. Is this true?"

With this, Melvin broke down and explained everything. That the drug was 2C-I and that Dean made it in his chemistry lab. This information was quickly relayed to me, and I went onto the Internet immediately and downloaded a structure and mass spectrum of this amine. The data on Kazumi was consistent with what I saw in these Internet reports. A week later, my lab purchased a 2C-I standard to verify the identity of the drug found in Kazumi's blood and urine.

*

Kazumi was no longer nervous as he stepped onto the stage in front of the cameras. He scanned the audience with his eyes. He did not know that the show's format had changed. Celia Lopez was now the only judge and he was going to sing directly to her alone! Unlike the audition, there was a full instrumental accompaniment. The music for his selected song began and the director signed him to begin. When he opened his mouth, no words came out. He looked over at the judge's table and was horrified to see that Dean was now sitting in Celia's seat. He had a smirk on his face. Then Kazumi woke up.

Kazumi's stroke produced irreversible brain damage. His mental and physical abilities were greatly impaired. Ultimately, he dropped out of school and became a dependent of the state.

*

Radiology and laboratory medicine have a lot in common as workers in both fields are providers of information for diagnosis and disease monitoring. Information from both fields was necessary in understanding what happened in this case.

Moyamoya is both an inherited and acquired disease. In

Japanese, "moyamoya" means "puffs of smoke." The disease was so named because angiographic images of these patients resemble smoke. "A tree has a trunk with large branches that get smaller and smaller as the tree grows," Dr. Zhang once told his radiology residents. "A shrub, on the other hand, may not have as prominent a trunk or degree of branching. It looks more like a continuum of twigs and leaves. This is Moyamoya Disease."

Women in their thirties and forties have a higher incidence of Moyamoya. In Japan, the overall incidence is 0.35 per 100,000. Patients with Moyamoya may have a series of stroke attacks. As primitive as it sounds, one treatment for this disease is to bore holes into the skull to allow for the growth of new blood vessels from the brain.

The "2C" family of designer phenylamines has about two dozen members, which all share the common property of being hallucinogens when ingested. They were first synthesized in the 1970s and 1980s by Alexander Shulgin, an American pharmacologist and chemist. Shulgin conducted studies on the effects of these compounds on himself and family members. He has written books about how to produce these amines and has described their psychedelic effects. Shulgin also popularized Ecstasy.

It was very likely that sooner or later, Kazumi's Moyamoya disease would have caused him to have a stroke. He had no way of knowing that the blood vessels in his brain were so small and diffuse. That he suffered from periodic headaches was the only clue to his anomaly. Dean and Melvin were not charged with their role in Kazumi's illness. Since Kazumi had a predisposition for a cerebrovascular accident, it could not be determined whether or not the drug itself was responsible.

I never met Kazumi, but saw his audition tape on American Talent. He could have been a recording artist, especially since there are very few Japanese-Americans who have achieved any success in that industry. At a minimum Kazumi could have been popular in Japan, just like David Hasselhoff is a popular singer in Germany.

Breast Report

****

Cindy Hartstein was the younger sister of Cathy, separated by three years. The two of them were very different. Cathy as very attractive and had an outgoing personality. Cindy was plain and reserved. Cathy was on the school's cheerleader squad and went out a lot, Cindy preferred to stay home and read. Like her mother, Cathy matured in her early teen years and eventually developed large breasts. This helped her gain popularity among the boys in school. Cindy on the other hand, was thin and had small breasts. Some of the boys in her class would tease her, wondering why she didn't have Cathy's shape. Cindy adored her sister and was never envious of her looks or figure. But as she grew older, the comments made by the boys caused her to become even more reticent and reserved.

Cindy went to a large public university majoring in information technology as a programmer. She spent hours of time on the computer learning languages and writing codes. She was more comfortable talking to her computer than to her roommates, classmates and other real people. The impersonality of the state school also suited her personality. The professors were too pre-occupied with their grants and research, and the counselors supervised too many students to take a personal interest in her. Besides, she got good grades and there was no reason that anyone would suspect that she would fail. Cindy graduated in four years and was near the top of her class. Cindy got a job at a large software company. She was given a small cubical and spent most of her work time on her computer.

When Cindy was in her mid-twenties, her mother Judy developed bilateral breast cancer at the age of 44. As all of her previous mammograms were negative, she skipped the last two appointments so it was several years since her last test. She was somewhat compliant with self-examination, but because her breasts were large, she wasn't taught correctly how to look for tumors. Her breasts were also dense which made it more difficult to detect by self-exam. During the workup of her tumor, it was determined that she was positive for estrogen and progesterone receptors, and overexpressed the gene for her-2/neu.

"What do all these test results mean" Cindy asked Judy's oncologist, a Dr. McNamara.

Dr. McNamara responded, "It means that she has a tumor that will likely respond to the adjuvant therapy that we are planning. The excess activity of the her-2/neu gene means that we can also use a special drug that only works on her type of tumor. You have an excellent chance of a prolonged remission after surgery" Dr. McNamara said. Judy underwent a total mastectomy on both breasts. After the surgery, she was given hormone treatment to reduce the odds of her breast cancer returning. Judy chose not to undergo plastic surgery to remodel and replace the breasts she lost.

"They always got in the way anyway" she said to Cindy referring to her breasts, trying to justify not getting implants.

Cindy did not have the same attitude and thought that her mother should have breast reconstruction surgery. Her parents had divorced years earlier. When asked about dating, she told Cindy "Now the men in my life will have to accept me for myself, and not because of what was on my chest" she said this proudly, but still with a tear in her eye.

Cindy was very happy at the success of her mother's breast cancer surgery, the positive outlook that the removal of her breast cancer gave her, and her acceptance of her new figure. But when someone told Cindy that there are some breast cancers that can be inherited, she became very concerned about her own health and that of her older sister. So she went on the internet and read dozens of reports. She quickly discovered one of the websites that was particularly relevant to Cindy and Cathy, and it was very disturbing.

*

Judy was monitored for her breast cancer by regular visits to her oncologist. Dr. McNamara uses my laboratory at the General for the various blood tests that she orders on Judy. Many of these tests are used to monitor breast cancer. One test in particular is CA 15-3, a protein that is released by some breast cancer tumors. A significant increase of CA 15-3 over time is suggestive of breast cancer recurrence or metastasis to other organs in the body. We followed Judy's CA 15-3 blood levels over the course of many years after her surgery for breast cancer. Judy's CA 15-3 values did not change significantly over time. Dr. McNamara explained to Judy that these test results along with her regular examinations indicated that her breast cancer was in remission.

In order to make the test results more assessable to the doctors and patients, we created a secure on-line clinical laboratory test reporting system. Using a specific login and password, a doctor can go onto our secure internet website to view and print out clinical laboratory reports on any of their patients. In this way, test results are available to physicians within minutes of the test's completion. This program greatly reduced the number of phone calls that we in the laboratory were receiving each day from doctors and nurses asking about a particular patient's test results.

The website indicates when samples are received and whether or not the test is complete or pending. Some doctors have also given access to this information to the patients themselves. This privilege is not granted to all patients, the doctor needs to determine if the patient wants to have access to this information and is able to understand the results. Judy was very involved with the management decisions made on her care and Dr. McNamara granted her permission to view her own laboratory results. Judy, in turn, trusted her daughter Cindy with her private medication information and gave her access to her test results as well.

*

In researching the genetics of breast cancer, Cindy learned that certain ethnicities can have a genetic predisposition towards cancer. In 1995, scientists from the National Institute of Health discovered the breast cancer gene BRCA1 and BRCA2. Women who carry mutations to this gene are at high risk for breast and ovarian cancer. Jewish women have the highest frequency of these mutations. Because Judy and her ex-husband were both Jewish, Cindy went through Judy's laboratory records and saw that this test was conducted on her. The proteins that are encoded by BRCA genes are part of a woman's defense mechanism against breast and ovarian cancer. Individuals who have mutations in both chromosomes for BRCA1 and/or BRCA2 have a greater likelihood for breast and ovarian cancer, estimated to be as high as 90% and 55% respectively.

In reading this information, a chill ran down her spine. Cindy quickly logged on to Judy's personal health record to review her mother's laboratory tests. Her computer was running slow that day. Loading, loading, loading..... was flashing on her screen. Come on! This is taking too long! Come on! she screamed to herself. After 1 minute, but what seemed like 20 to the anxious and nervous Cindy, the program was finally running and her mom's results were being displayed. Cindy scrolled through the many pages of results. She had looked at her mother's data before, but didn't know what they all meant. Now her heart was pounding like it had never before. Sweat came down her forehead. Finally, Cindy found the BRCA1 and 2 test results. Her mother carried the mutation that was the most likely cause for her cancer. Cindy knew that she was at high risk for the same disease as her mother. Cindy slumped into her and started to cry uncontrollably. She went into her bedroom and cried herself to sleep.

The next day, Cindy called Dr. McNamara to discuss the impact of Judy's genotype on her future health. "You are at high risk for breast cancer given your mother's history" Dr. McNamara told Cindy. But it doesn't necessarily mean that you have the mutation for the BRCA genes. Make an appointment with my nurse and we can have your blood tested. We'll then know for sure and we can discuss a plan on how you can reduce your risks for cancer."

Cindy came in the next day and had her blood drawn. We sent her blood sample to the same national laboratory that did her mother's testing. It was our practice to release a patient's test result first to their doctors and then to the patients after a 4-day waiting period. This gives a doctor the opportunity to review laboratory results before confronting their patients. We also have some laboratory tests that when values are above or below the "critical value," an automatic call is placed to the doctor.

These test results can indicate a life-threatening medical condition. For example, an individual with a very low blood sugar can become unconscious and comatose. The BRCA gene test was not on the critical value list, as this finding does not have any impact on the patient's immediate medical care. I would learn to regret not adding this test to the critical list.

Cindy was given access by Dr. McNamara to view her own laboratory reports. It would be a week before Cindy's BRCA results were reported to Dr. McNamara. Waiting was very agonizing to Cindy. She tried to keep her mind occupied with work, but it was very difficult for her to concentrate. Dr. McNamara was on vacation during the week that Cindy's results were posted on the internet. Personal medical news of this magnitude should be revealed to the patient by qualified genetic counselors who can thoroughly discuss the implications of the test and therapeutic options. A personal phone call to review lab results was the normal practice in Dr. McNamara's office. But the on-line reporting system was something new to her practice. Because Dr. McNamara was on vacation that week, nobody in her office saw the results prior to Cindy's access. So the patient was the first to see this important result.

Cindy was devastated by reading this report. She went back onto the internet to examine her options. She read that some women who have BRCA mutations were electing to undergo elective prophylactic surgery to remove their breasts and ovaries. Cindy also read about Angelina Jolie who had a well-publicized bilateral mastectomy due to her BRCA mutations and family history of cancer. *Angelina already has many children and will not need to have more of her own*, Cindy thought. She is also in her late thirties. Cindy was only 24 years old and hoped to get married and have children someday. All of these prospects seemed like a distant hope to her now. Cindy felt isolated and all alone. She wanted to call her mother but she felt that her mother was undergoing her own medical problems and didn't need to be burdened with something that may or may not happen. Cindy may have also felt that it was her mother's genetics that caused her to be in this situation. She called her sister but only got her answering machine. When the issue was brought up earlier, her sister was adamant that she didn't want to know about her own BRCA gene status. She told Cindy that she would never agree to a prophylactic mastectomy or hysterectomy in any case.

Cindy was highly distressed, which turned into a deep depression as the evening wore on. Although she didn't drink much, she went to her refrigerator in her apartment and drank several glasses of wine. Tired but insomnolent, she laid down on her bed and took a handful of sleeping pills. The medications were originally prescribed for her mother to treat her depression but Judy didn't need them so Cindy took them away. *I will face this issue tomorrow*, she thought to herself as she was swallowing. But Cindy was found dead the next day by her mother who came over when Cindy was not returning her calls.

The combination of alcohol and sleeping pills was listed as the cause of death by the medical examiner. There was no suicide note, as she did not plan to kill herself. On her nightstand was a copy of our BRCA1 and BRCA2 report indicating that she had genetic mutation that put her at high-risk for breast cancer. Upon hearing this story, my laboratory felt some responsibility for this outcome.

*

Our bodies are constantly exposed to harmful radiation and chemicals that damages our DNA. Without an effective DNA repair mechanism, cancer is one of the unfortunate outcomes. The BRCA genes encode proteins that assist in the repair of damaged DNA. There are dozens of mutations to the BRCA genes that reduce or eliminate the repair ability functions of the BRCA proteins. DNA mutations cause substitutions of bases that make up the DNA code. These substitutions encode different amino acids resulting in the creation of altered proteins. The mutation produces a protein that is no longer functional, as is the case for the BRCA proteins. Individuals with BRCA mutations are at high risk for development of breast and ovarian cancer.

A U.S. patent for the use of BRCA genotyping as a predictor of breast cancer was granted in 1995. Myriad Genetics, a reference laboratory was the exclusive licensee, and for many years, this was only laboratory in the US who could offer testing services without violation of the patent. A lawsuit was filed by the Association for Molecular Diagnostics challenging the right of a company to patent products of nature. In 2013, the US Supreme Court unanimously ruled that a naturally occurring segment of DNA was not subjected to patents. Competition for BRCA1 and 2 testing will reduce the costs for testing, and enable confirmation of results through a separate and independent source. "Second opinions" are a right of patients and a hallmark for medicine, especially for making important therapeutic decisions such as a prophylactic mastectomy.

In order to prevent tragedies like Cindy's case, my laboratory has a committee that determines which tests are considered sensitive and not subject to automatic release by software to patients. For example, tests that detect the presence of infectious diseases are not available, including those that are sexually transmitted. Due to medico-legal implications, viewing results for drugs of abuse testing is highly restricted. Tests that indicate a predisposition towards genetic disease, such as BRCA must also be accompanied by appropriate medical and genetic counseling. Every laboratory test has limitations in terms of accuracy and reliability. Therefore, laboratory test results must always be interpreted in the context of the patient's history and other findings by highly trained medical personnel.

Hair Today, Gone Tomorrow

****

Jennifer Sexton grew up in a small town of about 7,000 people. The biggest moment in her life was when she won her high school's Homecoming Queen title. She campaigned heavily for it. Seeing how she was not doing well in her classes, she felt that this was a better use of her time. She posted provocative posters of herself throughout the hallways to entice the boys to vote for her. She had large breasts and showed them off in these photos. The principal of the school thought these postings were inappropriate and had the janitors remove them after school. Unbeknownst to the principal, the pictures were moved to the custodian's lockers. Jennifer made more posters and new ones reappeared the following week.

Typically, not many boys ever voted for King and Queen. But this year, Jennifer's campaign resulted in a record voter turnout, boys included. The fact that her name was SEX-ton didn't hurt her chances either. Jennifer won the contest by a landslide. The King and Queen got to ride in the lead car in the homecoming parade and they had special seats at the football game. At the dance that night, Jennifer and the Homecoming King got the first dance alone. Everybody was watching them. They had been rehearsing this dance since they'd been announced as the winners. She personally didn't like the Homecoming King and she suspected that he was gay.

Jennifer's life went downhill after high school, as sometimes happens to people who live in small towns. Unless a small-town kid does well after leaving town, people stop talking about them. Jennifer was in that category, as nobody cared that she'd been the beauty queen in high school. Jennifer didn't go to college; she worked as a waitress at the local diner. She did not age well. Her skin had premature wrinkles. Men used to whistle when she walked by, but by the time she was in her early thirties, the whistling stopped.

Jennifer didn't have many marriage prospects. She ended up settling down with Clarence Dooley. He was a butcher, 12 years older than Jennifer. He was not attractive and had a dull personality. As the years went by, the thought of him cutting fresh meat off of carcasses each day increasingly disturbed her. But he made a good living and Jennifer was able to quit her job at the diner. Their sex life was good for the first few years. But as he became fatter and fatter, she lost interest.

"What was I thinking when I married him?" she remarked to one of her girlfriends. When their daughter, Crissey, was born, she didn't allow him to touch her anymore. They moved into separate bedrooms. By then, Clarence was nearing fifty and both of them lost interest in sex.

Jennifer devoted herself entirely to Crissey. She was a beautiful child. She had large green eyes and naturally auburn hair. Jennifer felt that Crissey could be a beauty queen just like she was when she was young. So she praised her daughter at every opportunity from the moment she could comprehend.

"Oh Crissey, you're so beautiful. There is nobody more special than you."

Jennifer did not let Crissey play in the park like the other children. "You'll just get all dirty. You don't want that, do you Crissey?" By the time Crissey was six, the neighborhood kids were calling her "Prissy Crissey." It was an accurate description. For fun, Jennifer dressed Crissey up in brightly colored pink dresses. She had her hair permed and adorned with bows. She wore high-heeled shoes. But she wasn't just wearing her mom's shoes, which would be too large and awkward to walk in. She owned her own fitted shoes. Jennifer spent a long time applying eyelashes, shadow, rouge, and lipstick to her daughter's face. She also got Crissey's ears pierced. Crissey cried when they were doing it, but Jennifer told her that it was necessary. She had big plans for her. She was just too young to know about it yet.

Jennifer wanted Crissey to compete in beauty pageants because of her looks and personality. But Jennifer resisted the temptation of entering her into these contests too soon. She enrolled Crissey in a charm school to teach her how to pose, smile, walk, talk, and hold her head straight.

"I wish my mother had given me this opportunity," she said to Crissey when her daughter turned ten. By that time, Crissey could see the advantages of being pretty and feminine. Jennifer told her that with her looks she could grow up to be a model or an actress. There would be fame and fortune. And they could both leave this one-horse town.

Crissey changed from cute to beautiful as she got older. When Crissey was 13, her mother decided that it was time for her to enter her first beauty pageant. She had the poise and charm needed to be successful. The beauty contest business is a rather small world. All of the girls, their parents, judges, and pageant organizers knew each other. So when Crissey Dooley hit the scene, she was a like a breath of fresh air. She was not a seasoned veteran like many of the other girls who had been doing pageants for many years and were largely participating just to please their parents. Unlike them, Crissey was genuinely excited by the competition and it showed.

Over the next three years, Crissey either won or was in the top three for almost all of the pageants she entered. Jennifer felt it was time for her to try the big one. Miss Teen USA. She told Crissey that this was what she'd been training for her entire life. Winning this title would give her college scholarships, modeling contracts, and television appearances.

"You'll be set for life," she told her.

Crissey thought about it differently. "I'll have the boys

chasing me," she said quietly to herself without her mother overhearing.

The first step was the regional pageant. Jennifer and Crissey checked into a hotel a few days before the event began. Many of the girls entering the pageant were older. Jennifer thought that if she had Crissey's hair highlighted, she would look more mature for her age. Jennifer asked the concierge at the hotel for the name of a reputable hair styling salon in town.

"A lot of girls go to the International Beauty Salon. It's just a few miles away," the concierge told her.

So Jennifer called and made an appointment for her daughter. The next day, they hailed a cab and walked into the salon to meet with the stylist.

*

Dottie Walsh was trained as a cosmetologist at a junior college. She hoped to open her own beauty salon one day. So she worked hard each day at the International Beauty Salon, saving as much as possible. Sometimes she would work a double shift when one of the other stylists wanted a day off. She didn't mind; she was the kind of person who only needed four hours of sleep each night. By the time she turned 30, she had performed haircuts, trims, permanents, and highlights on thousands of women. She could do someone's hair in her sleep.

Dottie had a boyfriend named Charles. She dated him off and on for the past nine months. He wanted her to move into his apartment with him, but she wanted a marriage proposal first. Both of them were very independent and both wanted to dominate the relationship. On the day that Jennifer and Crissey came in for highlighting, Dottie had an argument with Charles that morning. It was the usual fight about him not wanting to get married.

When Jennifer and Crissey arrived, Dottie was ready for them. Jennifer explained that she wanted streaks of blonde interwoven with her daughter's natural auburn color. She also wanted Dottie to style Crissey's hair and Jennifer brought pictures to show her. They agreed on a plan and Crissey sat down in the chair. Normally, Jennifer would have stood over Crissey watching every step along the way. But this time, she left the salon to see a seamstress about altering her daughter's evening gown for the pageant.

Jennifer picked up some teen magazines to read while Dottie went to the back of the store to prepare the hair chemicals and dyes. Dottie was taught that the hydrogen peroxide was unstable and had to be mixed with the bleach boosters just before applying it to the hair. While she was in the back room preparing the colorants, she got a phone call from her boyfriend. She took the cellphone from her pocket and answered.

"No, I told you I'm not interested in looking at apartments right now. I thought we settled this last night. Why are we still talking about this?" Dottie, not wanting to fall behind in her work, switched to her headset so she could still talk on the phone while preparing Crissey's chemicals.

"You know that I love you. This discussion doesn't change that." Some of her colleagues in the salon were listening with great interest to Dottie's heated discussion with her boyfriend. Crissey, on the other hand, was oblivious to the discussion and continued to read her teen magazine. "No. You know my terms. I'm not going to change my mind. Look Charles, I have to get back to work. I'll call you when I get home. Okay?" Dottie hung up and paused for a moment. She counted to ten to calm herself down. He's a scum bag. Momma was right. I can do better, she thought to herself. Dottie took the bowl containing the hair dye and brush and the foils went back to her client. The other girls in the salon could see that she was visibly upset, but nobody went up to console her. Dottie carefully brushed the chemicals onto Crissey's hair strands that were combed on top of the foil. She then carefully closed the foil around the dyed hair. She continued in this manner until all the highlights were added. Crissey was put under the dryer to complete the procedure. She was content reading her magazines and let Dottie do her work. Dottie got another call from Charles so she again went to the back room to talk to him.

Jennifer returned to the salon about 15 minutes later. She went over to Crissey to ask her how things were going. Crissey poked her head out from under the dryer and said, "Mom is it normal to have this burning sensation on my head? It's really beginning to hurt."

"What? Get your head out of there. That should never

happen. Dottie, Dottie? Get over here right now. What are you doing to my daughter?" Jennifer shouted across the salon. Dottie came running from the backroom. She quickly turned off the dryer and washed Crissey's hair in the sink behind her.

Jennifer demanded to know what happened. "There's nothing to worry about," Dottie assured her. "Sometimes there is some discomfort when we color hair. She'll be fine. Look, her highlights look really nice don't they?" Jennifer calmed down and saw that everything was fine. When Crissey's hair was blown dry, she admitted that she did look beautiful. She thanked Dottie, added a small tip to her payment, and they left the salon.

Crissey was stunning during every phase of the contest. She was poised and delightful. The judges loved her. Crissey ended up taking second in the regional Miss Teen USA contest. But as runner up, she would not be invited to the state pageant unless the winner was unable to attend. Jennifer was satisfied with this outcome. Crissey was only 16 and next year she would have a much better chance to win. When they returned home, the high school held an event to celebrate Crissey's success. Some of the old-time janitors were working and remembered when Jennifer looked just like her daughter. They still had her pictures although the images were fading.

Ten days later, Crissey's hair started falling out in large patches. She was horrified. Quarter-sized patches of dead follicles appeared on both sides of her head. This was the part of her hair that was bleached for the pageant. She went to school wearing a hat. Crissey and Jennifer met with a hair specialist who told them that there was significant scarring and that Crissey's hair would never grow back naturally. It was his professional opinion that individual follicle transplants of hair would not hold. She would have to have the skin of her scalp transplanted. This was a major operation requiring removal of her existing scalp and transplanting new skin. Crissey cried upon learning what had happened to her.

Jennifer contacted an attorney to discuss the potential of suing the salon that performed Crissey's hair highlights. Her medical insurance company denied coverage of the surgery that Crissey needed because they ruled that it was for purely cosmetic rather than medical reasons. Jennifer tried to argue that Crissey's future livelihood was at risk but they didn't agree. However, Jennifer believed that with a successful lawsuit, a settlement with the salon's insurance company might cover the costs for plastic surgery on Crissey's scalp.

*

Heidi Beck of the Wilson, Hamilton and Beck Law Offices found merit in Crissey's case and agreed to represent her. She said that they would have to find negligence in the salon's practices. Heidi needed a toxicologist who could determine if the hair dye chemicals could have caused the burning that Crissey experienced. So she called me, told me what happened to Crissey, and asked if I could help. I agreed and we talked about a plan.

The first thing I did was to find out which hair products were used on Crissey's hair. I sent my college-aged daughter into the International Beauty salon pretending that she wanted her hair highlighted. She asked the manager for the name of the products they used and if there were other brands that she could choose from.

The manager told my daughter that they had a contract with the supplier and these were the only products they used. Then he showed her the products. My daughter responded "I've used that product before, but I prefer Garnier," and she left without making an appointment.

Once I knew the product name, I went on line to look at the Materials Safety Data Sheets for each of the chemicals present in these products. The MSDS contains important information on all chemicals, compounds, and their mixtures that are manufactured today. These data provide useful information for workers who are exposed to chemicals in the workplace. If there are significant toxic exposures, the MSDS provides information on what first aid measures should be taken. The major components of hair coloring products are oxidizing agents, alkalinizers, hydrogen peroxide, and the coloring dye. Hydrogen peroxide has been used to bleach hair for many years. This liquid is usually used in 3% or 6% solutions. Persulfate accelerates bleaching and facilitates the absorption of dye by the hair. The oxidation reaction occurs at an alkaline pH and is facilitated by heat. When the hair coloring process is completed, the hair is thoroughly rinsed and washed with a neutralizing shampoo.

The MSDS listing for ammonium perchlorate stated that prolonged exposure may result in skin burns and ulcerations. The listing for 3% hydrogen peroxide warns users to avoid skin contact. The sheet for the alkalinizer, sodium metasilicate, stated that it is highly corrosive. Since it is a strong chemical base, I was not surprised to read this. I called Heidi and explained the dangers of hair dyeing to her.

"However, since most salons use these same chemicals, we would have to prove that there was some negligence that caused Crissey's injuries" I advised. "Otherwise, it would just be part of the risk of having this procedure done."

So on one of Dottie's days off from the International Beauty Salon, Heidi sent an investigator to the salon to speak with some of the other stylists. Those who were there that day remembered that Jennifer returned to the salon and started screaming at Dottie when she saw Crissey in pain. They also told the investigators that Dottie was distracted by phone calls from her boyfriend. Heidi believed she had the foundation for a negligence case. She filed a lawsuit against the International Beauty Salon. They did not go after Dottie Walsh herself, thinking that she didn't have any money. Heidi subpoenaed Dottie for a deposition in Crissey's case. Heidi, lawyers for the beauty salon, and a court reporter gathered in Heidi's law office.

"What time did you start the procedure?" Heidi asked Dottie.

"The appointment was at 2:00 p.m. Crissey and Mrs. Dooley arrived on time. Mrs. Dooley left on an errand around 2:15."

"How long was Crissey under the hair dryer?"

"No more than 15 minutes."

"Was it on low or high heat?" Heidi asked.

"We always use low heat," Dottie responded.

"I have an affidavit from Mrs. Dooley swearing that the heat temperature was in fact on the high setting," Heidi said. "She was there when Crissey started to complain and was the one who turned off the dryer. She remembered that she turned the dial two clicks to the off position, not one click as would have been required had it been on the low setting. You were not there when Mrs. Dooley arrived back from her errand. We also have witnesses who have stated that you were in the back room on the phone arguing with your boyfriend. Do you deny these events?"

Dottie admitted that she was distracted that day but had done hundreds of hair highlighting procedures before and never had a problem.

As a test, Heidi then asked Dottie to name each substance used in the hair dye procedure. Since Dottie was saving money to open her own salon, she knew more about the business than any of the other stylists. She was able to list the ingredients one by one.

"Potassium persulfate, sodium metasilicate, and 9% hydrogen peroxide," she recited. Seated in the deposition room, I asked Heidi to request a brief break so that I could confer with her. The deposition took a short recess.

In the hallway, I told Heidi, "The normal hydrogen peroxide percentage is 3-6%. They used a 9% solution, which is not recommended by the cosmetics industry. That fact, along with the increased hair dryer temperature, and Dottie's inattention to her client during a critical stage of the procedure, contributed to Crissey's injuries, in my opinion." Heidi fully agreed.

Heidi Beck thanked Dottie for her deposition and dismissed her. Heidi then asked for a recess and held a private conservation with the defendant's attorneys. She pointed out that there was both a deviation from accepted hair dying practices and negligence by the stylist. The bad publicity of this case would ruin the salon's business. The salon owner decided to settle the case with no admission of guilt. The two sides agreed on an appropriate dollar amount. Jennifer accepted the offer and the case was settled. Crissey had hair transplants to restore her bald spots. It would be years before she entered a hair salon again. She lost interest in participating in any more beauty pageants, much to the dismay of her mother. Crissey just wanted to be a normal teenager.

Dottie Walsh never got the salon she was hoping for. She married a businessman and retired as a stylist. Crissey finished school and was the first in her family to go to college. She was still very pretty. Jennifer divorced the butcher. He was secretly having an affair with a woman who worked at a delicatessen next door. They shared many more common interests with each other than he had with Jennifer.

*

In 2001, an expert panel published a report on the safety of ammonium, potassium, and sodium persulfates, accelerants used in hair dyeing products. The report concluded that these chemicals were safe for use on consumers if proper procedures were used. The key was limiting exposures by reducing the incubation period, eliminating heating, and thoroughly rinsing the chemicals from the hair at the earliest opportunity. There have been cases of subjects having allergic reactions to the dyes used on their heads, but most of these reactions have been temporary and non-debilitating.

A larger concern by the panel was the constant exposure hairdressers have to these chemicals. Repeated inhalation of vapors can cause asthma. Contact dermatitis can result in rashes and allergic reactions. Patch tests conducted on the skin of salon workers can be used to verify the allergen. Individuals susceptible should select another line of work. At all times, gloves must be used when handling dye solutions.

Crissey Sexton's hair loss highlighted the need for tighter oversight of beauty salon practices. Stylists and manicurists experience occupational exposures to chemicals that may be harmful to them over a prolonged career. Thinking about exposure to harsh chemicals reminded me of my college days when I took classes in organic chemistry. Repeated exposure to organic solvents was a principal reason why I chose not to pursue a career in synthetic chemistry. Thirty years ago, repeated exposures to organic fumes probably shortened the lives of chemists. Fortunately, that's not the case today.

Mr. Potatohead

****

It started out innocent enough with Barry. He was five when his parents let him watch the movie, *Close Encounters of the Third Kind* on their old VHS recorder. Although the movie was rated PG, this was probably a bad idea given the child's age. Fortunately Barry did not understand the alien invasion theme of the movie, and was only fascinated with the scene where the Richard Dreyfuss' character, Roy, is piling mashed potatoes high onto his plate. In the movie, the aliens were directing Roy to sculpt the spuds into the shape of Devils Tower in Wyoming, the site of the alien encounter. Barry laughed and laughed when he saw this scene. His parents thought Barry's reaction was amusing. He asked his parents to rewind and show this scene over and over again. Unfortunately, from that moment, Barry became obsessed with eating various forms of potatoes and playing with raw ones. It was as if the aliens came across the screen and brainwashed Barry, just like they did to Roy and the other characters in the movie. His mother thought her son had some psychological affliction and wanted to send him for professional help but his father thought he would eventually grow out of it. Barry did temper his affliction during his teen years largely because his friends would pick on him about it. But alone and at home, he still craved all forms of potato products. At breakfast it was hash browns, at lunch, Breast fries, at dinner, baked, mashed, or au gratin. There were potato chips in between, plain, barbecue, ripple, or sour cream, it didn't matter. Everyday, it was some form of potatoes. It was like Bubba's obsession with shrimp in the movie *Forest Gump*. Only for Barry, it was potatoes; and this was real, not a movie. There would be no restaurant franchise in his future. At least at that point, he was not making mashed potato mounds with his food. He was just eating it.

Barry went to the state college, met Chloe in an accounting class and married her. Chloe became a Certified Public Accountant and Barry became an actuary at an insurance company. It seemed to be a good match at first. Barry's job did not require him to have significant interactions with anyone outside his immediate office. While his co-workers saw that he liked potatoes, no one thought it was an affliction. Chloe, however, saw this obsession getting worse over the years and it affected their marriage. She tried to get counseling for him, but he refused, they eventually got divorced over it. It may have been one of the few cases where irreconcilable differences were over a vegetable.

Once alone, Barry could fully exercise his potato addiction unabated. He transitioned from cooked to raw products. He was eating up to 3 pounds of raw potatoes per day, skin and all. He had a particular predilection towards green potatoes which were hard to find in a grocery store. So he learned that if he exposed fresh potatoes to the sun, they would turn green through photosynthesis.

In addition to his obsession with eating potatoes, he also began to exercise curious eating habits. In his mind, he divided his plate into four equal segments along the face of a clock. Before eating, he carefully divided his food into each of these quarters. He would always begin eating with the 12 o'clock segment completed before beginning with the food near the 3 o'clock segment. By the time he reached the 9 o'clock segment he was nearing the end of the meal. But instead of using a fork, he took the plate to his face and licked the food directly off the platter, making slurping and sucking noises with each swipe of his tongue. Given this ritual, Barry could no longer eat in restaurants or even in front of friends or guests without ridicule. This behavior ultimately turned him into a recluse. He stopped eating out at restaurants. He found a source of raw potatoes that were sold wholesale in 100-pound bags to restaurants. These sacks were automatically delivered to his house on a quarterly basis. Barry's affliction went on for years before anyone besides Chloe knew there was a problem.

Then one day after a large potato meal, Barry's fetish caught up to him. Barry suffered severe diarrhea, nausea, vomiting, and stomach cramps. This never happened to him before. Although his symptoms became worse over the next few weeks, Barry did not stop his peculiar diet or habits. He started having nightmares, hallucinations, and muscle spasms. He was sweating profusely. One evening, he stumbled out of his apartment, took a few steps, and passed out onto the floor of the corridor. Nobody in the apartment building heard him fall. It was a few hours before his neighbor came out of his apartment and saw Barry lying there. The neighbor called an ambulance and Barry was taken to the emergency room at the General Hospital. Contained within his wallet was his mother's telephone number as his only emergency contact. He hadn't spoken to her in several months. When someone from the ED staff asked if her son had any unusual drug or chemical exposures, she said no. But then after a few moments, she did say to the caller, "My son does have some unusual eating habits. Could this have something to do with his problem today?" None of the doctors in the ED knew if this was important or relevant. The assignment to find out more about this was given to Vivian Nagumo, a fourth year medical student.

*

I got the call from Vivian on the second day of Barry's admission. She told me about a patient who may have overdosed on eating potatoes. I asked her to repeat what she said but I heard it right the first time. I didn't know that potatoes could be toxic so I too did some investigation. Some species of potatoes contain solanine, a glycoalkaloid. Botanists have long known that solanine has fungicidal and pesticidal properties. Through a natural selection process, these plants evolved through natural selection to become part of the plant's natural defense mechanism against bugs and microorganisms. In mammals, glycoalkaloids can inhibit cholinesterase activity, an important enzyme found in the axon of neurons. Nerve cells communicate with each other through the release and uptake of neurotransmitters such as acetylcholine. Cholinesterase converts acetylcholine into inactive choline and acetic acid thereby returning the neuron back to its resting state. Inhibition of this enzyme causes cholinergic symptoms such as excess sweating, tears, and secretions. It can also produce excessive muscle contractions, the result of overstimulation of nerves that are connected to muscle.

Individuals exposed to a class of pesticides known as organophosphates will produce cholinergic symptoms similar to those that Barry exhibited when he was admitted to the ER. Nerve gases such as sarin are also cholinesterase inhibitors. These poisons have been used as chemical weapons by terrorists. In 1995, members of the Japanese cult Aum Shinrikyo released sarin gas from canisters into a crowed Tokyo subway during rush hour, killing 13 people and seriously injuring dozens of others. Many of these victims had symptoms very similar to Barry's. Vivian remembered this event, as she lived in Japan as a teen.

*

Barry's blood and urine samples were sent to my

laboratory at the General Hospital for testing. We have two procedures for measuring the cholinesterase activity, one found in red cells termed the true cholinesterase activity, and the other found in water or the serum part of blood termed pseudocholinesterase activity. Both of these tests are used to monitor agricultural workers, such as those in the central valley of California who are exposed to organophosphates. Field worker are exposed through the spraying of vegetables with these pesticides by crop dusters. In Barry's blood sample, we found an abnormally low cholinesterase enzyme activity in both his red cells and serum. This confirmed that his symptoms were likely due to his exposure to a chemical or drug that inhibited this vitally important enzyme.

The abnormal cholinesterase test was consistent with the symptoms Barry exhibited. It was then necessary to determine the underlying cause. Given Barry's history of overeating potato-containing products, we sought to find the levels of solanine in his blood at the time of his symptoms. It took us a week to find and purchase the appropriate standards, develop the solanine assay, and perform the analysis by mass spectrometry. We were able to find published testing methods in the food testing industry. In these reports, the scientists use the same instruments and methods that we use for testing blood from our patients. Although blood concentrations are much lower than what is found in potatoes, we have high sensitivity equipment that enabled us to find very low concentrations of these compounds in the blood and urine samples. Eventually, we were able to confirm in Barry's blood a toxic level of both solanine and chaconine, another alkaloid found in tubers.

*

In the emergency room on the day of admission, Barry was treated with atropine which quickly relieved his symptoms. Barry was then sent to a psychiatric facility where he underwent a full evaluation of his food fetish and counseling for this disability. Barry was 35 years old and willingly admitted himself to the facility. Maybe he should have gone when he was a kid or as an adult when Chloe suggested it. Nevertheless, he knew now that he needed help to rid himself of this addiction. Our analysis that directly linked solanine toxicity to his illness was useful to the treating psychiatrists.

After careful evaluation, his doctors diagnosed Barry with the DSM-IV code 307.50, "Eating disorder, not otherwise specified." The DSM-IV classification scheme of mental health diseases was established in 1994 by the American Psychiatric Association. Barry's particular disorder was characterized by "extremely atypical eating behaviors that are not characterized with either anorexia nervosa or bulimia nervosa," the more common of the DSM-IV eating disorders. He was also diagnosed with code 304.90, "Other substance-related dependency."

An established medical diagnosis enabled Barry to take a medical leave of absence from his employer with full pay and benefits. While at the psychiatric hospital, his diet and access to food were carefully controlled. It was very difficult for the first few months as he had a terrible craving for potatoes. Fortunately for him, his addiction was psychological and not a physiological chemical dependency. After 5 months, he was discharged and Barry returned to his job. His co-workers knew he had been hospitalized and were happy to see him back. Barry maintained regular appointments with his psychiatrist, Dr. Vivian Leblanc.

Six months after Barry's discharge, Vivian presented his case to faculty and students at the monthly ED lunch conference. Vivian asked Barry to attend. While bringing in the actual subject of a case that is being discussed is highly unusual at a medical conference, Vivian wanted to show the doctors who cared for him that Barry was open in dealing with his psychiatric affliction and was recovered. He was applauded by the doctors for his appearance and perseverance. He avoided the chips that were served with the sandwiches to the residents and fellows in the audience. Vivian apologized to Barry afterwards stating that it was not a test, and that she had nothing to do with the catering that day. Nevertheless, Barry passed the test.

*

There are over 1 million acres of land in the US that are devoted to cultivating potatoes, with each acre yielding over 40,000 pounds. The states of Idaho and Washington combined are the largest producers in the U.S. The average American eats 140 pounds per year. One third of the potatoes are used to make French fries, one quarter is sold fresh, and 15% are made into potato chips. Potatoes, tomatoes, eggplant, peppers and other vegetables contain steroidal glycoalkaloids and are part of the nightshade plant family. Prior to the 1800s, these plants, especially tomatoes, were considered poisonous. Today, tomatoes consumption is cherished for its lycopene content, a carotene (but not a glycoalkaloid) that has anti-cancer properties.

Regarding potato toxicity, large amounts of potatoes must be consumed before any symptoms appear in most individuals. The highest concentrations of solanine are found in the leaves, stems, and shoots. When the tuber itself is green, consumption should be avoided or minimized. Death due to potato poisoning is extremely rare. In 1933, an outbreak in Cyprus killed 60 people. During the Korean War, some 20 subjects died in North Korea. The incidence of poisoning by potatoes is likely underreported by physicians because gastrointestinal symptoms are more commonly caused by bacterial or viral contamination of food. However, the presence of cholinergic symptom is suggestive of the presence of a cholinesterase enzyme inhibitor. Exposures to chemicals such as parathion and malathion occurring among farm workers is more common than potato toxicity. Through regular surveillance and the move towards growing crops organically, the incidence of pesticide and herbicide toxicity has declined over the last few years.

As a child, my mother always told me to never eat the sprouts of a potato. When she was preparing meals, she was careful to remove potato eyes with the end of the peeler. I always thought that this practice was silly and unnecessary. While she might not have known the chemical basis for her admonishment, I now know she was right.

Purple Reign

****

Having an interest in both world history and science fiction, and having been a clinical laboratory scientist for over 30 years, I have often played the "what if" game in my mind. I am particularly fascinated with how medical illnesses among key world leaders influenced the course of history. If we could go back in time to diagnose illnesses and apply modern medical treatments to key individuals from the past, it would create a ripple effect that would change our very existence today. Many take for granted the freedoms and liberties that we enjoy in our country today. Could this reality be altered if key decisions in history were changed?

One such individual that played a large role in the formative years of American history is George III, who became the King of Great Britain and Ireland at the age of 22 years and ruled from 1760 until his death in 1820. King George was a central figure in the Revolutionary War which began in 1775. King George was 37 years old at the time. The war was started by the American colonists who were being taxed by the British government but had no representation within Parliament. Colonists felt that they were simply pawns to the will and whim of bureaucrats across the Atlantic. As the war continued and casualties mounted, George's cabinet ministers thought that the King should consider the colonist's demands. However, George III was adamant in fighting the rebels until ultimate victory was achieved by the Empire. He felt that giving in to the colonies might spark revolution and independence among the other British colonies. Of course, Britain lost the war and the colonists gained independence from the British in 1783. With the loss of the 13 colonies, the British Empire set their sights on securing neighboring Canada and the exploration of the Pacific. Just before the Revolutionary War, James Cook discovered the eastern coast of Australia. A few years after the end of the war, Britain established "Botany Bay," and sent exiled English convicts to New South Wales in Australia. There were no wars of independence between Britain and Canada or Britain and Australia. They eventually formed their own Parliaments. However, both Canada and Australia remain members of the British Commonwealth and are ceremoniously ruled by the Queen of England.

History has shown that King George suffered from recurrent mental illness. He became seriously ill in 1788 to the point that he was unable to fulfill many of his royal duties. Granted that this was after the war, but if he had a genetic disease that caused this illness, he may have been sick a decade earlier. Centuries later, psychiatrists and physicians have suggested that

George suffered from an inherited metabolic disease. Did ill health cloud his judgment during critical times of his reign? How might the world look today had he been diagnosed and treated appropriately? The following is an account of history re-written with the availability of modern clinical laboratory diagnostics and therapy.

*

George succeeded to the throne when his grandfather, George II died in 1760. Within a year, he married Charlotte of Mecklenberg-Strelitz, whom he met on their wedding day. Within a year, their first son was born who was heir to the throne and later became King George IV. George III and Charlotte ultimately produced 15 children. Their marriage was a happy one. Unlike his predecessors and descendants, George did not have any mistresses.

George's health was good until he began suffering from attacks when he was in his early 40s. His symptoms included severe abdominal pain, muscle weakness, and numbness in various parts of his body. There were also skin lesions and blisters on his arms and legs. The King was also agitated, depressed and suffered from hallucinations. These attacks would coincide with upsetting news regarding the 13 colonies in America that he was getting from his foreign ministers on a weekly basis. They thought that the King was having panic attacks. This didn't make sense to his chief physician, Dr. Henry Beauregard, because King George was used to political instability, and regularly dealt with issues within his government and abroad. The Royal physicians suspected a medical problem and did a thorough physical exam of the king, which included a regular analysis of his urine. The doctors knew that sugar in the urine was a sign of diabetes and had laboratory workers whose job it was to taste the King's urine to see if it was sweet. His urine was clear and devoid of any glucose. In contrast, when he went into one of his psychotic fits, his urine would be a bluish purple in color. Dr. Tarpley Cox was one of the Royal doctors involved in the King's care. He had just given a lecture on urine testing to his students at the London Royal Academy of Medicine.

"Normally, urine has a yellow colour due to the presence of urobilinogen, a pigment produced in the liver by the breakdown of hemoglobin. Red-colored urine can be caused by kidney injury or disease and is due to the release of red blood cells and/or hemoglobin. Red urine can also be caused by eating certain vegetables such as beets or rhubarb. Dark urine can be caused by extensive muscle injury and is due to the presence of myoglobin, which is another oxygen-bearing protein containing heme. When the urine is white or cloudy, it may be due to the presence of bacteria which can be the result of a urinary infection."

Dr. Tarpley had never seen purple urine before. So he went to the archives to find if anyone published on this before. While searching the medical literature is a simple matter today, back in the 1760s, there were no computers, internet, search engines, or printed catalogs. There were only a few medical journals. But after several days of searching, he was successful in finding an article in the "Philosophical Transactions of the Royal Society," a journal first published in 1665 by the Royal Society of London. The article described a patient with purple urine, just like the King. The article further described the investigation as to the cause of this pigment. Dr. Cox also read about Vlad Tepes III Dracula, the Prince of Wallachia in Transylvania, who lived some 300 years earlier. Dracula was most healthy when he stayed out of the sunlight and in the dark of night. He had a thirst for liquids. Modern day folklore suggests that this liquid was blood *Hmmm,* Cox thought. *Perhaps the King and Dracula have the same affliction?*

A few days later, Dr. Cox met with Dr. Beauregard and his staff met to discuss what his research showed.

"Heme is an iron binding molecule that is the active part of hemoglobin" Dr. Cox remarked. This is essential for red blood cells to transport both oxygen to the tissues and carry away carbon dioxide as a byproduct. Heme is produced from porphobilinogen through a series of enzyme-catalyzed reactions. If any of these enzymes are defective, high levels of porphobilinogen is excreted into urine. Because this molecule is reddish-purple in colour, individuals with acute porphyrias produce urine that has this hue. There is a simple test that we can conduct to determine if the King's urine contains this metabolite. We add a solvent and chemical known as the

Ehrlich's reagent. If porphobilinogen is present, the solution will turn a red rose color."

Impressed by his investigation, Dr. Beauregard granted permission to Dr. Cox to have this test done on King George's fresh urine sample. The extraction of the urine by the organic solvent produced a colorless liquid. When the Ehrlich's reagent was added, the red color instantly appeared indicating a positive result. Dr. Cox rushed to report his finding to Dr. Beauregard. Satisfied that the King was suffering from the disease same disease as Dracula, the next logical question was how should George be treated? Dr. Cox noticed that the lesions on the King's skin got worse when he was exposed to the sunlight. He told Dr. Beauregard that the King should avoid direct sunlight exposure unless it was absolutely necessary. When he was outdoors, he should have as much of his skin covered as possible.

"We can't expect the King to be a hermit inside his own castle" was Dr. Beauregard's response. "He has duties to the kingdom and his subjects."

"Then let me keep track of the times and days when he is outside and what the weather conditions are on those specific days." Back then as today, London has periods of many days and even weeks without significant sunshine. "If his lesions improve during the rainy weeks corresponding to less sunlight exposure, this might corroborate my theory" Cox concluded. Dr. Beauregard saw no harm in this plan and agreed. The young doctor's time was not as valuable as his.

After one month of observation, Dr. Cox's theory proved to be correct. Skin lesions appeared on days when the King was exposed to sunlight, and resolved during long periods of overcast skies. His demeanor also appeared better on rainy days. When Dr. Beauregard, who took sole credit for this observation, told the King of the potential dangers to his health from the sun, the Royal Highness opted to reduce his outdoor exposure. When it was necessary, he wore ceremonial clothing that covered as much of his skin as possible.

The king was also instructed to drink as much fluid as possible. Dr. Cox reasoned that the porphobilinogen was a poison and that it should be flushed from his body as quickly and efficiently as possible. Drinking water that contained sugar also facilitated thirst and more frequent urination. While he didn't know why, the King's diet rich in carbohydrates also reduced the frequency and severity of his attacks. Fortunately, he did not crave for blood as Dracula had. All of these measures appeared to work. The King was more relaxed and exhibited far fewer symptoms than before and he was back to his happy self. As a result, the King fathered several more children during this time.

Ultimately, King George's personality and outlook changed from one of aggression to one of peace and calm. When the colonists begin to complain about their treatment by his cabinet, the King took a very different approach toward them rather than what actually occurred in history. The King decided to negotiate with the colonists rather than wage war. All but a few of the militant colonists who wanted independence from Britain, were thrilled. Most of the colonists were simple farmers and merchants and did not want war with the mother country. The decision by the King to negotiate rather than fight dramatically changed history from that point forward.

Within 6 months, Benjamin Franklin, who was 71 at the time, sailed to England to become the first representative to the British Parliament. General George Washington, who was the hero of the Revolutionary War, was the head of the colonial army. But since there was no war, he did not become the first President of the United States and his name was not significant in the history of the country. Four years later, Thomas Jefferson replaced the aging Franklin in Parliament. By then, the 13 colonies were known as the "United States of New Britain." The name of the town of New Britain, Connecticut, which predated the formation of the USA, was changed to "America", Connecticut.

Eventually the United States of New Britain became a nation separate from Great Britain. The New Britainers elected their own prime minister instead of a president, and created their own parliament instead of a congress. The U.S. of N.B. remained a commonwealth of the United Kingdom, along with Canada, India, and South Africa. With an emphasis on maintaining relations with U.S. of N.B., England did not explore or colonize Australia. It became a separate country and continent unrelated to the British Commonwealth. It was inhabited by the Japanese instead and was called "Australasia." As a commonwealth nation, the New Britainers entered World War I at its inception in 1914, instead of a few years later in 1917. This infusion of solders ended the war two years earlier. Not only did this save millions of lives, but the blame and reparations that Germany felt after the war were minimized accordingly. Rampant inflation did not occur, and as a result, Adolf Hitler did not rise to power, and there was no World War II, no holocaust, or mass causalities. The world's population inflated to 10 instead of the 7 million it is today. There was also no need to develop rockets or nuclear weapons. The absence of German rocket scientists delayed the development of the US and Russian space program for a half century. Nuclear power as an energy source was also delayed.

Even popular culture changed dramatically as the result of the singular decision made by King George to keep the peace. The two American pastimes of football and baseball became soccer and cricket. In Australasia, instead of rugby, Sumo wrestling became popular under the Japanese influence. Words like "apartment" and "elevator" were replaced with the British words "flat" and "lift."

All of these changes were made possible by a young physician who made medical observations and influenced the treatment of a king in a manner that was different from convention and what actually occurred in history.

*

The suggestion that King George III suffered from acute porphyria was made in the 1960s by two psychiatrists Dr. Ida Macalpine and her son Richard Hunter, who examined medical records and other documents relating to the period when the King became ill in 1788. According to records, the King experienced bizarre behavior, peripheral neuropathy, muscular weakness, vocal hoarseness, abdominal pain, and he excreted urine that was discolored. These investigators also corroborated their opinion by citing that current descendants of the King have evidence of porphyrias. In 2005, scientists found a high concentration of arsenic in the King's hair and they suggested that this metal disturbs heme synthesis thereby the precipitating porphyria attacks. The King's hair was provided by the Science Museum of London. The source of the arsenic was thought to be the medications his physicians were giving him. Recently, other scientists have reviewed the Macalpine and Hunter data and refuted their findings.

The Watson-Schwartz screening test for detection of porphyrin disease is one of the older clinical laboratory tests in existence and was developed in 1941. The test is still used today. The Ehrlich reagent that is used in this test was first discovered in the 1880s to stain hemoglobin. Naturally, neither this reagent or the lab test existed in the mid 1700s at the time of King George III's reign. In fact, porphyrias, as a disease was not described until 1874 by Dr. Schultz. The term "porphyrin" comes from the Greek word "porphyus, a reddish-purple color. Today, we have genetic and precise biochemical tests that can identify the specific cause of porphyria in any given patient. We cannot know if history would have been changed with the availability of even the earlier science of porphyrias.

Some may feel that this story and the one that follows are silly since this technology was not available for over 100 years. However, is it more likely that we will have time machines that can take us back to those times and alter history, as has been the theme of some movies and books.

Bladder Control

****

It was Sunday night in Washington DC. A man who aged dramatically over the past 4 years stepped in front of the television camera. He was addressing the nation from behind the desk of his office. He spoke about peace in a region that suffered civil war for 20 years. He spoke about his efforts to stop the bombardment of a country and its people. He spoke about his need to devote his time toward the duties of his office and not his responsibilities to his political party, in this election year. The date was March 31, 1968. The man from Texas then stunned the nation with his concluding remarks:

"Accordingly, I shall not seek, and I will not accept, the nomination of my party for another term as your President."

After he finished the remainder of the speech, he stepped away from his desk at the Oval Office and away from camera view. There, he met and hugged his wife, Lady Bird. She could see that a big burden was lifted from his shoulders. A tear came to her eye as she knew it was the beginning of the end of a long career in public service. She recalled the sacrifices that he and their family made. There were many hours of negotiations with his colleagues from both parties. She remembered the criticism he and his administration suffered. The man knew, however, that there would be difficult months ahead for him and his country. There was some satisfaction that somebody else would be making these difficult decisions soon. The burden of responsibility was simply too much for him and it was time to pass the torch.

As can be imagined, this speech immediately sent shock waves to key members of both political parties. This was especially true for the incumbent party, as they naturally assumed that President Lyndon Baines Johnson would seek a second full term. Nevertheless, several prominent members of the Democratic Party indicated their desire to run for president and they entered state election primaries prior to the President's March 31st speech. These candidates campaigned on an anti-Vietnam War platform, given that the President's approval rating for the war effort was at an all-time low. But in reality, these candidates were simply positioning themselves for the 1972 election.

Notably absent from candidate considerations in 1968 was the incumbent vice president, Hubert H. Humphrey. Humphrey was a liberal democrat who sought the Democratic nomination in 1960 but failed then because he didn't have the financial assets that Kennedy had. Now as the Vice President, his liberal followers were dismayed that he did not publically oppose the President's policies on the war. While not widely known at the time, Johnson threatened to withdraw his support of Humphrey's future presidential aspirations if he didn't support the current administration's foreign policies. When Johnson withdrew from the 1968 election, Humphrey needed to decide if he was going to enter his name as a candidate for the Democratic Party, and if yes, would he pledge to continue the current Administration's commitment to the Vietnam War effort or withdraw the troops from the conflict once elected. Humphrey waited a month before formally announcing his candidacy. He also decided not to break with the President's policy on Vietnam.

Humphrey was well behind the other candidates, notably Eugene McCarthy who won the Oregon and Pennsylvania primaries, and Robert Kennedy who won in Indiana and Nebraska prior to Johnson's announcement. Four days later, Kennedy won the California primary and was well on his way to the Democratic nomination.

Humphrey, was at his apartment in Chevy Chase Maryland watching the returns on the television. When he learned that Kennedy won, he turned off the set not wanting to hear his victory speech. Humphrey was awakened by an aide in early morning of the next day telling him that RFK had been shot and killed in Los Angeles. The nation was recovering from the assassination of Martin Luther King in Memphis just two months earlier. Humphrey went to the bathroom and just before flushing the toilet, he noticed a red color in the bowl. He didn't know what this meant, but didn't bother to tell his wife or any of his staff. *Today is going to be a very long day,* he thought to himself, *and I don't have time to worry about what this means.* He met with his campaign staff to discuss the length of mourning that was appropriate for the death of Robert Kennedy. That night before going to bed, he noticed that his urine was no longer red. *This morning must have something I ate,* he thought to himself.

The campaign resumed in earnest in late June, as the candidates were preparing for their party's nominating conventions. At that point, Humphrey was second in the polls for the Democratic nomination. From the Republican Party, Richard Nixon was nominated in early August. The Republican convention was uneventful compared to the Democratic Convention held in Chicago later that month. There were demonstrations and riots in the streets by students and dissidents protesting the war. Humphrey succeeded in capturing the Party's nomination over McCarthy amidst the chaos of the convention. That night, he noticed blood in his urine for the second time. When he returned to Washington, he called Dr. John Wagner, his private physician, and asked to be examined.

While at the doctor's office, Humphrey provided another urine sample that was as bloody as the one from the previous evening. Dr. Wagner told him that there were dozens of reasons why blood can be present in urine and that the laboratory would need to do some testing. Satisfied, Humphrey got dressed and his driver took him back to his office in the Executive Office

Building.

The urine sample was sent to the National Cancer Institute in Bethesda. I was a postdoctoral fellow at the time the sample arrived in the clinical chemistry laboratory. Privacy laws referring to medical histories were not as they are now, and everyone in the lab knew that the sample was from the Vice President. It was not uncommon to receive samples from noted politicians in Washington. It was quickly confirmed by the laboratory that Humphrey's urine contained blood and other cellular substances. The sample was centrifuged and the cells were sent to the Dr. Lloyd Dubois, a noted expert in urine cytology. Dr. Dubois and colleagues at NCI recently discovered p53, the tumor suppressor gene that produces a protein that helps in repairing DNA. His studies showed that a high number of individuals with mutations to the p53 gene have a genetic predisposition to acquiring cancer. The presence of blood in the urine with this mutation suggested that Humphrey may have the early stages of bladder cancer.

It was two weeks before Dr. Dubois had laboratory confirmation sufficient to warrant a call to Dr. Wagner. When the Vice President received the news from Dr. Wagner, he was in denial.

"I feel fine. There have been no other episodes of bloody urine since" Humphrey told Wagner. It was a lie. Humphrey would occasionally see blood but this was not a time to be worried about his own health.

"Nevertheless, I'd like to start you on some experimental chemotherapies that are being tested at Memorial Sloan Kettering in New York. Some of these doctors were involved with the initial discovery of p53" Dr. Wagner pleaded.

"What will this do to my stamina?" Humphrey asked.

"It will make you tired. You will likely lose your hair. You may need to take some time off to have this done" Dr. Wagner stated.

"John, I'm running for the Presidency of the United States. We are less than 7 weeks from the election and I am 15 points behind Richard Nixon. This is not the time for me to step away from the campaign. I must make a final push for the White House. There is no time for the Democratic Party to find a replacement. We are the incumbent party!" Humphrey said.

"I know, Hubert. But as your doctor, I am obligated to tell you that your best chance of survival is to get treated for the tumor now, while it is in its early stage. You are no good to the country if you are dead" Wagner pleaded.

"We're in crisis right now. Students are protesting in college campuses across America. Fanatics have killed Martin Luther King and Bobby Kennedy. George Wallace is threatening to bring back school segregation. We started this, I cannot stop now." With that, Humphrey started to get dressed to leave. As he was departing he said, "I expect you to maintain our patient-doctor confidentiality. I will see you after the election."

"Of course" Dr. Wagner said as the Vice President was

leaving. "God be with you, Hubert" Wagner said after Humphrey left the office.

With the potential diagnosis of bladder cancer, Hubert Humphrey saw his own mortality right before his eyes. He had devoted most of his life to public service, starting as the mayor of Minneapolis in 1945. Shortly after his visit with Dr. Wagner, Humphrey assembled his campaign team. They urged him to denounce Johnson's Vietnam policies in favor of de-escalation and ending the war. In the past, he consistently told them that he would not back-stab his friend and colleague. But on this day, his aides could see that he showed a new resolve. He informed them that they were to change their campaign. He was throwing caution to the wind because of his imminent mortality and returning to his roots of pacifism.

In his first campaign speech after this meeting with his staff, he told the stunned audience that if he was elected president, he would immediately stop the bombing of Hanoi. He also devised a plan to gradually withdraw American troops from Vietnam. Win or lose, he was going to end the war once and for all and he repeated this at all of his campaign stops from that point forward. Humphrey was more energetic and driven than ever before.

November 5th was election day in 1968. The real history saw that Humphrey lost the popular vote to Richard Nixon by just 500,000 votes. Because Humphrey distanced himself from LBJ earlier, history was changed. Humphrey and Edmond

Muskie from Maine took office in January of 1969. True to his word, the Humphrey administration stopped the bombing of North Vietnam and negotiated peace terms which led to the withdrawal of troops. The last soldiers left in August 1971.

It was a year from his first meeting with Dr. Wagner that he returned to his office for a checkup. At that point, his bladder cancer had progressed to Stage III. Humphrey underwent radiation and chemotherapy but it was insufficient to stop the spread of cancer to his liver. Doctors at the National Cancer Institute opined that the stress of the President's office led to an accelerated progression of disease. Humphrey died in June, 1971. Like Franklin D. Roosevelt, he did not live long enough to see the end of the Vietnam conflict. Muskie was sworn into the presidency and completed Humphrey's term. In 1972, he and George McGovern from South Dakota were nominated by the Democratic Party and won the election. Their Republican opponent was Ronald Reagan, governor of California.

*

This story diverged from the true history at the point when Humphrey's urine was being analyzed for cancer. It is accurate that the Vice President did have blood in his urine, but it was in 1967, a year before he announced his candidacy for the 1968 presidency. While the cells from his urine did reveal a mutation in p53 and a diagnosis of bladder cancer was evident from that test, the protein was not discovered until one year after his actual death in 1978. With permission from Murial Humphrey, laboratory testing was conducted in 1994 from samples that were taken in 1967 and were archived by the pathology laboratory. History showed that Humphrey lost the 1968 election by the narrowest of margins in history to that date, a difference of only 500,000 votes. This was largely because he waited until the end of September to distance himself from LBJ. Even with only 5 weeks to go, the Democrats closed the gap with Nixon and on Election Day, the polls were even. Political analysts have stated that if the election was a week later, he would have been voted into office.

In this story, because a laboratory test revealed a high likelihood of bladder cancer, Humphrey departed from Johnson's policies two weeks earlier. This was sufficient to tip the balance in his favor during the 1968 election. A change of just 177,000 votes out of 73 million that were cast that year in 4 key states (Illinois, Missouri, Ohio and New Jersey) enabled him receive the required electoral votes to win the election, despite still losing the popular vote. This story highlights how the course of American history from the Vietnam War to modern day may have been altered if this single lab test had been available. The withdrawal of troops by the Humphrey administration in 1969 would have resulted in the savings of over 10,000 American lives.

Fat Rescue

****

Fanny Deerfield was 72 years old when she needed knee replacement surgery. She had advanced arthritis and could barely walk. She was told that with a knee replacement, she could go ballroom dancing again with her husband.

Fanny was scheduled for the elective procedure on a Tuesday. Prior to the procedure, she went in for baseline blood tests, which showed no abnormalities. She was cleared for the surgery. Fanny was instructed to arrive at 6:30 am for a 10:00 a.m. surgery appointment. Her daughter took the day off from work and drove her to the General Hospital. Dr. Carlton Davies was the orthopedic surgeon scheduled to do the procedure. He had done thousands of knee and hip replacements over the years and was very confident and experienced. Dr. Len Drasnick was the anesthesiologist assigned to the case.

"Bupivacaine is a local anesthetic widely used for these types of knee replacements," Dr. Drasnick told his students who were in the operating room witnessing the procedure that day. "It has a good safety profile when the correct intravenous dosages are administered."

As part of the plan, Fanny was supposed to be awake and conversant during the surgery. Her consciousness was important to monitoring the progress of the procedure. But after a few minutes, she became restless, agitated, and incoherent. Her blood pressure dropped and she developed a tonic-clonic seizure while on the surgery table. A few seconds later, Fanny's electrocardiographic tracing was flat lined. Her face turned a pale gray. She was having a cardiac arrest. The surgeon, Dr. Davies, backed off and looked directly at Dr. Drasnick, who immediately recognized this situation as cardiac toxicity due to the anesthetic drug he administered. He initiated cardiac compression that was quickly followed by defibrillation. Dr. Drasnick called the nurse to bring in the cardiac arrest crash cart, which was nearby.

Calmly, the nurse asked, "Should I prepare an ampule of epinephrine, doctor?"

"No!" Dr. Drasnick replied. "We are going to administer 100 milliliters of 20% Intralipid." Dr. Davies was baffled. He knew nothing about treatment with Intralipid, but trusted Dr. Drasnick, who proceeded with the injection.

Within a few minutes, pulses and electrocardiographic signals returned. Fanny's color also returned to a familiar red/pink. Fanny Deerfield returned from the dead! Because of the arrest, the operation, which hadn't begun in earnest, was terminated. After it was clear that her medical condition was stable, Fanny was wheeled into the recovery room. Her daughter was notified that the surgery needed to be postponed but that her mother was fine.

In the scrub room, Doctors Davies and Drasnick were cleaning up and changing. Dr. Davies approached Dr. Drasnick to find out what he had done to so quickly to reverse the medical emergency.

"Len, I don't believe in miracles, but you seemed to have performed one in that operating room today," Dr. Davies marveled. "Tell me, how did you know that Intralipid would work? And why is it even in the OR?"

They sat down in the break room so Dr. Drasnick could explain. Dr. Davies already knew that Intralipid was a fat emulsion solution widely used at the General Hospital and elsewhere to treat patients who were unable to achieve adequate nutrition by eating. The current formulation was a solution of soybean oil, egg phospholipids, and glycerin, and was administered intravenously.

Dr. Drasnick then explained that the use of Intralipid as a rescue for anesthetic drugs was discovered quite accidently. They both knew that some of the best medical discoveries were made in this manner. Scientists were trying to figure out why some patients develop heart toxicity while on bupivacaine, a drug known to disrupt the body's energy production. If fatty acids, known to be toxic, accumulate as a result of bupivacaine, it might explain how this drug causes harm. So a research study was conducted on rats to test this theory. Laboratory animals were pretreated with Intralipid containing these acids or a placebo prior to bupivacaine expecting toxicity in the treated rats. What the scientists found was quite unexpected. The Intralipid-treated animals actually did better, not worse than the animals who received no lipid treatment.

Dr. Davies was listening with great interest.

Dr. Drasnick continued, "So an anesthesiology colleague of mine recently had a patient who was in cardiac arrest after bupivacaine, similar to our case today. The patient was not responding to epinephrine rescue, and he was quickly losing the patient. He was familiar with the Intralipid animal research studies and asked for Intralipid to be brought to the OR, where he performed the first infusion of Intralipid rescue ever attempted on a human. The patient's cardiac condition dramatically improved and he survived."

Dr. Davies replied, "Wow, that colleague of yours took a big chance medico-legally, being the first to try using Intralipid off label."

"Yes, but it was a controlled gamble," Dr. Drasnick replied. "He believed that the patient would not survive anyway so they were desperate to try anything. You know this as well as anyone, Carlton, sometimes you have to just do what you must in order to save a life. I've seen you do some unconventional surgical maneuvers that prevented a major bleeding catastrophe or repaired an unexpected anatomic anomaly."

"You're right," Dr. Davies said, "Sometimes you just

have to think outside the box."

Dr. Drasnick continued, "Besides, Intralipid has been used for decades here, and the safety profile is well known. No one has ever suffered any major complications due to Intralipid. Maybe some isolated allergic reaction cases. Since that cardiac arrest case, which was presented in our anesthesiology meetings last year, there have been others who have successfully used Intralipid to save patients. Our Society has now recommended that Intralipid be put on crash carts just in case of these emergencies, which is why it was here today."

Dr. Davies admitted that he hadn't heard about Intralipid rescue and didn't know it was used at the General Hospital. "This is actually our first case," said Dr. Drasnick.

"Just how does Intralipid work?" Dr. Davies asked.

"We're not really sure. The best theory out there is that the presence of Intralipid in blood preferentially binds to fat-soluble drugs, thereby extracting them from their tissue sites. I've discussed this with the director of our chemistry laboratory here. He and his students are doing a research study to determine if Intralipid can bind anesthetic drugs and other medications from human serum in a controlled laboratory study. They're scheduled to present the results to us sometime next month. In the meantime, I'll contact him and tell him about our case so he can do some retrospective follow-up on Mrs. Deerfield. But we already know it worked today."

*

Dr. Drasnick met with me about Intralipid months before the Fanny Deerfield case. Once I heard about the cases outside of the General Hospital, I jumped at the idea of expanding the research study with assistance from one of my students, Deb Ireland. In addition to studying bupivacaine, I asked Deb to identify other drugs that were listed by the American Association of Poison Control Centers' National Poison Data System as having the highest incidence of toxicities, including other pain medications, anti-epilepsy drugs, antipsychotics, and stimulants. She tabulated the expected serum concentrations of these drugs from poisonings published as case reports, and she developed assays to measure drug concentrations in serum. The Intralipid protocol involved spiking serum with drugs, adding Intralipid, centrifuging the sample to remove the fat layer, and measure how much drug remained in the serum. The "Intralipid Extraction Coefficient" was computed from the before-and-after Intralipid treatment. We found that some drugs were efficiently removed by Intralipid, while others were not.

When the bulk of the data was completed, I challenged my students, "We need to establish a model based on a drug's chemical or physical properties that will allow us to predict its extraction efficiency by Intralipid." They knew from me that clinical toxicology was unlike other medical disciplines. "You will never get ethics committee approval to drug overdose a patient in order to see if a particular therapeutic management approach will be effective. Our knowledge is sometimes based on experience by others in similar clinical situations. It would be great if we could have some objective data."

So Deb Ireland and I attempted to correlate the extraction efficiency against each drug's attributes. Chemical parameters included the acid/base strength, molecular weight, water and fat solubility, melting and boiling points, and volatility. We also examined pharmacokinetic factors, which relate to the characteristics of drugs in the human body, including how much drug was distributed into plasma, known as the volume of distribution, its half-life, the degree of binding to plasma proteins, and the drug's clearance rate by the liver and kidneys. After extensive mathematical modeling, one parameter stood out above the rest: the drug's lipid partition constant, i.e., the tendency of a drug to bind to fat. The higher the number, the more likely treatment with fat will work. Sometimes the answer was the most obvious choice from the list of variables examined, but my team tested all factors.

"So the percent agreement between the lipid constant and the actual lab findings is 88%," I stated from reviewing the group's analysis. "Once our work is published, a clinical toxicologist who is considering emergency therapy by Intralipid for a drug overdose can have some expectation as to the success or failure of the therapy. Of course, our in vitro model may not necessarily translate to the same degree of extraction removal in serum from a real overdosed patient. We will know in time if some of the drugs that we predict will work with Intralipid actually do, once they are used."

Our study was presented to a clinical toxicology meeting and published in a reputable journal. Most of the clinical scientists stated that the data was sound and logical. Several groups have subsequently duplicated some of the drugs that were tested by my research group. There were other variables that have to be considered when using lipid for drug treatment.

"There are different Intralipid formulations depending on the specific product," I remarked to a colleague after my presentation at the meeting. "In the U.S., Intralipid contains triglycerides with long chain fatty acids. In Europe, lipid emulsions of triglycerides containing medium chain fatty acids are used. These products will have to be separately tested for their efficacy in removing toxic drug concentrations."

*

More than half a world away in Melbourne, Australia, Talbot Tankersley was in a hospital for four months after being involved in a motorcycle accident. While he was recovering from his injuries, he started to get nightmares. He was diagnosed as having post-traumatic stress disorder, which was a common complication. He was prescribed sertraline to relieve these symptoms. This appeared to relax him from his anxieties sufficiently enough that after two weeks he was discharged from the hospital. After another two weeks, Talbot returned to his job as a landscaper for the large animal pavilion at the city zoo. There, Talbot met Nancy, who was working at the concessions stand. Nancy was a quiet girl, with red hair. She had a great smile and a lovely personality. They started dating and she eventually moved in with Talbot. But after six months, Talbot and Nancy started arguing because she wanted to go out more often. He explained that he was still recovering from his bike accident. Eventually, Nancy moved out. She continued to work at the zoo, but avoided talking or seeing Talbot while at work.

Talbot still had feelings for Nancy and hoped he could get back together with her. But then Nancy started to date Horace, one of the zoo's finance managers. Talbot became jealous of Nancy's new boyfriend. One Friday after work, he went home to his apartment feeling particularly depressed. He bought a six-pack of Foster's and sat down to watch Australian football on television. But he couldn't get Nancy off his mind. The alcohol made him feel more uninhibited than usual. He grabbed his bottle of sertraline and swallowed an overdose of pills with the beer.

This will get her attention, he said to himself.

After a few minutes, he became dizzy, his heart started racing, and his body started shaking. His apartment was spinning around his brain. He began hallucinating and hearing voices. It was Nancy and Horace pointing their fingers at him and laughing. Talbot became psychotic. He ran out of his apartment and into the hallway screaming.

"Stop it! Stop it! Leave me alone!" he shouted. He then passed out and hit his head on the floor. Someone in the apartment building heard the commotion and went outside to the corridor. Talbot was lying face down and was unconscious. An ambulance was called and he was back in the same emergency department where he was after his cycle crashed.

The medical resident in the ED was Lachlan Smedley. In Talbot's pocket was an empty bottle of sertraline. The emergency response team reported that Talbot was seizing en route to the hospital. Talbot's blood pressure was extremely high at 200/120. Dr. Smedley determined that Talbot's symptoms were consistent with an overdose of sertraline. The doctor ordered activated charcoal, which was quickly administered. But the patient remained comatose: Glascow Coma score of 3. Dr. Smedley wasn't sure what to do next. He then remembered an article he read from America regarding Intralipid rescue. In fact, he remembered that it was used successfully for treating a tricyclic antidepressant overdosed patient in Sydney, earlier in the year. So we went online, downloaded our published article and found out that sertraline was one of the drugs that was successfully removed by Intralipid, at least in test tube experiments. So he called the pharmacy and ordered 100 milliliters of 20% Intralipid. It was intravenously infused into Talbot's left arm. Within 10 minutes, it appeared to improve the patient's condition. Talbot's symptoms gradually resolved over the ensuing hours. A repeat infusion was performed four hours later, in case there was any residual absorption of the drug from his stomach.

Dr. Smedley called the clinical laboratory and asked that

leftover blood from Talbot's routine electrolyte testing be retained for future analyses. Dr. Smedley told the lab that he would be contacting me to see if my research group would be interested in testing these samples in conjunction with this case. He reasoned that it was our data that prompted them to try this rescue in the first place. Talbot was kept in the emergency department overnight to ensure that there were no residual drug effects.

Word got out at the zoo that Talbot was sick and in the hospital. Nancy and Horace came to visit him. They brought with them a live baby kangaroo to help cheer him up. It was wrapped in a blanket so no one knew what it was, but a nurse saw the animal and asked that it be taken outside. Once they'd left, Talbot realized that he'd missed his chance with Nancy, but told himself that it was time to move on. Maybe next time, he would be more committed to a longer-term relationship. He realized how stupid he'd been, and he was grateful to be alive.

Dr. Smedley found my email address from my last article and sent me a message. He was hoping that I would collaborate with him in writing a case report for publication. He didn't have a laboratory to do any research of this kind. I read his email a day later, and was elated to learn that our work might have helped someone. I emailed him back to let him know that I would definitely be interested in receiving blood samples. We found that the concentration of sertraline was initially very high in Talbot's blood. The blood sample collected after Intralipid administration resulted in a reduction in sertraline concentration of over 50%. A smaller percentage drop was observed after the second bolus of Intralipid. When our analysis was completed, Dr. Smedley and I published a report on the Talbot rescue.

"Future doctors may benefit from this experience if a similar overdose case occurs again with sertraline," I wrote in an email to my Australian colleague, after the paper first appeared in an e-publication ahead of print. "Intralipid or variations of this product can be found in almost every hospital in the world. It is very inexpensive. To have a new tool for treating drug overdoses, with the antidote already in our back pocket, is truly amazing. We only need to make this information more known to the medical world. Then we need doctors like you to have the foresight and nerve to use it."

*

In the United States and throughout the Western medical world, commercial Intralipid products approved for total parental nutrition (a means of feeding through a tube) are now standard issue for cardiac arrest crash carts for the off-label treatment of patients who have toxicities to anesthetic drugs. This mandate was driven by anesthesiologists, who were the specialists that originally discovered this use. Clinical toxicologists, having learned of the success of this therapy, are now using Intralipid rescue for other drug poisonings. Ideally, our studies done in the lab that suggested which drugs would be rescued by Intralipid needs to be validated in real poisonings. However, controlled animal studies to determine fat rescue success, such as that conducted for bupivacaine, are impractical to perform for every drug that can result in a human poisoning. Moreover, these studies would be difficult to conduct, as there are no current agencies willing to financially support this work. For now, use of Intralipid for novel drug poisonings will require some faith and risk by caregivers that such an approach will work in addition to, or in lieu of, conventional medical management paradigms.

Few doctors will freely admit that they overdosed a patient with an anesthetic drug. The availability of Intralipid rescue provides a safety net for these occurrences. This new therapy may prove useful in the non-surgical setting, i.e., overdoses of other drugs and medications, either accidental or purposeful. Whether or not Intralipid becomes a mainstay for the treatment of emergency department overdoses remains to be seen.

Epilogue

****

The clinical laboratory is an essential part of medical practices today, affecting all specialties. There are over 4000 "in vitro diagnostic" tests available to physicians and their patients. Testing is conducted over 7 billion times per year in the US alone. Lab tests are the least expensive component of medical care, yet it has been estimated that lab test results affect more than 70% of all medical decisions that are made. Like drugs, the medical indications for lab tests are reviewed and approved by the Food and Drug Administration. Clinical laboratories are regulated by the Centers for Medicare and Medicaid under the Clinical Laboratory Improvement Amendment.

Despite its vital role, the importance of the clinical laboratory and the professionals who produce results is underplayed by the medical profession. For example, there is no structure for teaching laboratory medicine during the first year of didactic training. Instead, students learn about lab tests when they enter the clinical phase of their training, on hospital wards. Their education on what lab tests to order is taught by residents and senior medical students who themselves are not properly trained. Practicing on real patients is not the ideal time to first learn about what lab tests are. As a result, there are significant errors in terms of what should be ordered and when. Incorrect orders lead to wasted resources and unnecessarily drive up the cost of medical care. More significantly, as highlighted by stories in this book, errors in the interpretation of lab results can lead to significant patient morbidity and mortality.

The ignorance of clinical laboratory tests extends to the general public as well. Most patients blindly accept that the tests ordered on themselves are appropriate; patients don't question the need for the tests or understand how they are used. This is slowly changing with access to the internet. Many resources are available to patients and their families to learn about lab tests so they can take some responsibility for their own medical care. One of the most popular web sites is Lab Tests on Line (**http://labtestsonline.org/**). This free on-line resource allows users to type in the name of a test, to retrieve information on how it is used, and when and learn how it is ordered by physicians in managing their patients. They can also enter the name of a disease or disorder to discover what tests are typically ordered for that condition. Most doctors encourage a discussion regarding their patient's medical care. Studies have shown that an informed patient is much more likely to be compliant with therapy than those who are ignorant.

We all want what is best for ourselves and our loved